Also by DJ Geribo

Novels
The Mart
Useful Pieces

Short Story Collections
Deep Lake House
Seven Storied Houses

Non-Fiction
Me & Them
The Miracle Dog

Children's Books
Mouse Bound
Eddie Easel and the Case of the Missing Green
The House at the Top of the Trees

Both the publisher and the author encourage you to purchase directly from www.BBDPublishing.com as this supports the author in the most direct manner.

You can also ask for many of the author's works directly from your favorite bookseller.

Select titles are available on Amazon in paperback and Kindle formats.

TEN
STORIED
BUILDINGS

TEN STORIED BUILDINGS

DJ Geribo

BBD Publishing ~ Alton, NH

Ten Storied Buildings is published by

BBD Publishing
P.O. Box 351
Alton, NH 03809

www.BBDPublishing.com

Book Layout and Editing by James J. Fontaine

Cover Design by Positively Creative Solutions, LLC

Printed in the United States of America

10 9 8 7 6 5 4 3 2 1

Library of Congress Control Number: 2025926643

ISBN 978-1-970715-00-2

To all the people who work at these jobs or live these lives, you are always my inspiration.

TABLE OF CONTENTS

Ten Storied Buildings

The Church

Barbara sat on the hard wood bench and let her thoughts roam. She thought about the hard bench, especially as she has aged and doesn't have the padding she once had. Made of oak, smooth with no ragged splinters to catch a skirt or pants on, layers of polyurethane creating a shine while guaranteeing many years of daily use. But why so hard? Couldn't they at least add a long cushioned piece to cover the cold solid seat? But people didn't come to church to be comfortable. Most came to the high-ceilinged hall with long stained-glass windows, marble floors, rows of hard wood benches, and a coldness to the atmosphere that brought a chill to your bones to alleviate some kind of guilt they held inside, hoping for forgiveness. And seeking forgiveness was never about comfort.

But Barbara did come here looking for comfort. And answers. Mostly answers as to why her Benjamin was taken at the young age of sixty-three, after just retiring from a job he gave forty-two years of his life to, why him? She knew there were mean people in this world and she heard how many of them lived far into their eighties and nineties. People who were abusers to their spouses and to their children. Murderers, rapists, wife-beaters, terrorists, child-molesters, the list goes on and on. Take them, not her Benjamin, a loving husband to her and their two children. He deserved a good life for many more years. And her, what about her? She did the best for her husband and her children and now she is suffering also. Fairness, for her it was about fairness. Taking a wonderful man way before his time was not what he deserved.

And this was the main reason that brought her to the church and brings her here every day seeking answers to all these questions she now has. She never was an extremely religious person, didn't make her kids go, just when they were younger but then thought they should find their own way after that. Occasionally Benjamin wanted to go, mostly after he lost a parent or a family member or a good friend. But once he was taken from her too soon, she needed answers. She spoke to a priest at this church and he said what he learned to say to people who are grieving. The usual, 'it was his time', 'God needed him to come home', 'he's out of pain now and in a better place'.

It wasn't his time and God didn't need him, she needed him. He wasn't in pain and the best place he could be was home with her. Just pat answers they told everyone without knowing anything about the individual's circumstances. They would say the same thing about the child-abusers and wife-beaters. What, after all, would a priest know about a man who had married a woman and had a family with her? He knew nothing about the love they felt for each other and their children. How could he advise her about anything? He asked her to come back again, he did see she was in pain, but he didn't recognize that mostly she was getting aggravated with the empty answers he passed onto her as if they would give her comfort. He might as well have been reading a recipe out of a cookbook.

She really didn't expect much from the church. But still, she found herself dressing and walking the half mile to the big building that smelled of musk incense. She did like that smell. Maybe that was where she found her comfort, in an aroma that reminded her of the time she met Benjamin. It was at a concert with a few hundred people. They were both waiting for the port-a-potty and as they waited, they started talking, asking where each was from, what was their favorite rock band, what kinds of food they liked. When one of the three port-a-potties became available, he let her go first. Then he went in and she waited for him to come out. There was an immediate connection and she didn't want it to end. When he came out and saw her standing there, his entire face smiled at her and he reached for her hand as they walked back to the concert together. But neither seemed interested in the concert any longer and after trying to carrying on their conversation, Benjamin asked if he could give her a ride home and she said 'yes', informing her friends that she was getting a ride from him. Her friends, a bit more cautious, wondered if it was a good idea. He gave her friends his license plate number, his name and address, and even the place where he worked and his boss's name and phone, plus his mother's name and phone number. He figured he had all his bases covered and her friends finally agreed to let her go with him, threatening that if anything happened to Barbara, they would hunt him down like a dog. Benjamin then thanked them and after shaking hands with Gail and Simon and Lesley, took Barbara's hand and walked to his car. She immediately loved his car, a big Oldsmobile Cutlass, pale blue, with cushy leather seats. He put a blanket across the seat for her and said, "I know leather can be chilly so you might like the blanket on the seat." She smiled, nodded and slid over towards Benjamin's side, but not too close. She didn't want to appear fast but she felt so comfortable with him. And his hands, she absolutely loved his hands. They were warm and strong and looked like they worked hard for a living.

First impressions can be lasting and Barbara relived that first meeting with Benjamin again and again. Even more so once he had passed. But she had so many wonderful memories with Benjamin. Ones that she knew had to last the rest of her life. Because there wouldn't be any more. This was it.

It had been three months now since Benjamin was taken from her. Three long, hard months. Her wonderful children helped as much as they could but they had to work and they had their own families to care for, too.

Barbara stopped this path of sorrowful thinking because it always led to the same scenario — her collapsing in tears, curling up in bed, falling asleep from exhaustion. And she couldn't do that mostly because she was in church right now. She had to distract herself and decided to look around at the other poor souls who made their way into the ostentatious building. Why, she wondered, such high ceilings? Why so many solid gold statues and she was positive they were solid gold because nothing but the best for the disciples who followed the bible and other religious scripture. Such a waste. People are starving, why all the frills? Especially since the priests and nuns lived such frugal lives but they are surrounded by wealth and people love donating to churches, apparently buying their way into heaven. This was good, she giggled, since it was getting her mind off the sadness that seemed to grow like a tumor inside her.

Her favorite place to sit was just outside the confessionals, about half-way down from the front, on the left side of the church. Confession was from ten to noon and from two to four pm. She wondered why such limited time to listen to people confess their sins. Wasn't this why they were here? What else did they have to do all day except pray, why couldn't they give more time to their congregation? Priests who give sermons, I guess they have to write their sermons for the next day. But does that take all day? Aren't there plenty of guilt-soaked sermons to throw at the congregation that could be written up in a matter of minutes? I mean, the list of sins that people commit is endless and surely each sermon will reach those who come here for forgiveness, prompting them to reach deep into their pockets, hoping with each dollar they drop in the collection box that they can continue to climb that stairway to heaven where they will be invited in with open arms, when their time comes. She wondered, too, if she was one of the few who was coming here for answers, not forgiveness. She had no interest in sharing whatever sins she may have committed in her lifetime with complete strangers, better known as 'the priests'. It was none of their business. Her sins, committed during her lifetime, were between her and her conscience. And when he was alive, between her and Benjamin. If he was ok with how they lived then so was she. Also, she had been taught the difference between good and evil and neither she nor Benjamin had committed any evil act that came even close to some of the sins that the Catholic church and the men they hid from the public eye had committed over the years. So why would she confess anything to one of their representatives?

She changed her position and slightly turned to look to her right and at the back, where a lot of single individuals tended to sit. She was sure some were just looking for a place to sit down, get out of the cold, especially in the winter months. Others, she noticed, just wanted to sleep. How they could curl up on these hard as rock benches was a mystery. There were two or three others who, like herself, showed up every day at about the same time she did. She wasn't sure if they paid any attention to her, she was mostly lost in her own thoughts and barely noticed the others. One woman in particular had her rosary beads and mostly kept her head down. Barbara could see her mouth moving so she figured she was praying. Does someone, a woman in particular, have that many sins that she has to come here day after day and try to pray her sins away?

Another woman was more interesting to Barbara. She changed her seat every time, sitting all the way at the back or right up in the front bench. Sometimes she moved into the very center of a row, other times she sat at the ends. Almost as if she was trying to find the best possible place for God to see her, or maybe for her to see God. Or maybe she was trying to get the attention of a priest who was sometimes up at the altar, changing the linens that covered a few of the tables, adding more candles, taking away ones that had burned down too low, or finding other chores to attend to. In the winter there was snow to mop up. Occasionally someone vomited and the priests also had to clean that up. Although they did all this without pay, she knew they were all well taken care of and had no bills to worry about. She also knew that with their focusing on the church and finding more people to convert and brainwash into following their religion - in particular Catholicism, the only choice someone should make - that they really didn't know much about the real world or family life in particular.

Barbara shook her head, her thoughts bringing her back to why she was here and what she was looking for from God in general, and these priests in particular. After two and a half months of daily visits to this church, she wasn't any closer to knowing the answer to why her Benjamin had been taken.

"It is so peaceful here, isn't it?" The voice, so close to her, caused her to jump and stare into the face of the mover. How she never saw her heading this way surprised Barbara and her first thought was to shoo the woman away. But she was also curious about the woman and her travels through the church, almost like one switching lanes on the highway. Was she trying to get someplace? And where exactly was that?

"Yes, yes, it is peaceful. Is that why you come here?" Barbara really was curious about this woman and why she moved around so much. She decided to start slow.

The woman muffled a laugh, smiling beneath her leather gloved hand.

"Oh, you noticed. Yes, I do move a lot around the church. I just like to see everything from different perspectives. I'm an artist and perspective is everything to me. Not that I'm going to paint the inside of a church." Now her laugh escaped and she put her gloved hand tightly over her mouth and then, looking over her shoulder and at the front of the church, checked the other patrons as well as the priest, who was no longer at the altar. Barbara also smiled. And now she liked this woman even more and her first thought of 'interesting' now changed to 'intriguing'. She wanted to know more.

"I'm Barbara. Barbara Jenkins."

"Hello Barbara Barbara Jenkins. I'm Sally Machetti." Barbara snorted and now she put her hand over her mouth and looked around the still quiet church. She suddenly felt like a child misbehaving and waited for a nun to shush her and Sally.

"Just Barbara. One Barbara. So, is that like the knife?" Of course, she had to stifle another laugh thinking about the movie 'Romancing the Stone' and Just Joan.

"No, like the Italian restaurants all across New England."

"Oh, fabulous, I love that restaurant. Didn't realize there was more than one."

"There are twelve restaurants, all owned by members of the Machetti family – we do our best to overpopulate the planet."

"Do you have children?"

"I do not. I don't even have a husband. I have my art, that is all I have ever wanted." Barbara thought how nice to not have to worry about money, to have a successful family to pay rent and for food and clothing.

"And before you think my family handed me this life on a silver platter, I've worked for everything I have. I was supposed to go into the family business but I went to Art school instead, switched in my second year. That was enough for my parents to basically disown me. I teach at the community college and I paint the rest of the time. Have art shows and sell my art for big bucks."

Now Barbara was impressed and regretted her thoughts going to where most people would go, that Sally's life was easy and everything was given to her. She couldn't believe she did that and almost apologized to the woman. But then she realized they were her thoughts and she hadn't actually spoken the words out loud.

"Well, you should be very proud of yourself. I am and I don't even know you."

"Thank you, that is very nice."

They both sat quietly for a while, each lost in her own thoughts about the conversation they'd just had, each wondering where to go from here. Barbara shivered, suddenly realizing that the place was like a tomb, cold and unwelcoming. She really could use a cup of tea.

"Would you like to come back to my place for a cup of tea? I live walking distance from here."

Sally seemed to hesitate, then slowly nodded her head.

"Or, if you'd rather not, we can just be satisfied with the pleasant conversation we've just had. I haven't had a good laugh in a while, I do appreciate that."

"Oh, no sorry - I mean, yes, I would love to. It's just that I'm working on a piece for an upcoming show and was wondering if I can spare another hour or so. I've already stayed past my allotted time here."

"Or, we can make it another time?" Barbara didn't want the woman to know how desperate she was for the company of another woman. Although it was obvious Sally was a good fifteen or more years younger, she was fun to talk to and Barbara had always found creative people more interesting to talk to; they usually had the most amazing stories to tell. It was a world she, at one time, had wanted to work in. But when she'd met Benjamin, everything in her life had changed. She'd never thought about going back to her writing. She used to love to write poetry and was sure, if she dug through her boxes of letters, that she had at least enough to put into a book and maybe even see if she could publish it. She had started writing a poem about Benjamin and their life together but it was just too sad. Although, she thought, weren't most poems sad? The ones she'd read over the years were usually sad tributes to someone they'd loved and lost, or who'd left them and broken their heart. Maybe when she'd been a child, she'd read some happy poems but, as an adult, there was so much heartache that the poets all sounded like they were on the verge of committing suicide. She just didn't want to make her life all about the sadness even though that was the emotion she found herself enveloped by right now.

"Ok, let's do it now. Maybe just a short visit. I need to get out of my studio and go somewhere besides church. Although, I do love the quiet here, and the incense; there's something about that smell, I guess it reminds me of childhood and going to church. But then, that should make me run from the place because I don't have the fondest memories of the nuns and how strict they were with children, children for God's sake! Sorry, I'm rambling. So, yes, I can drive us to your place. You said you live close by?" Sally took a breath and waited for Barbara to respond.

Barbara quickly took a mental inventory of her refrigerator, hoping she had milk and at least some cookies to offer Sally. Or, maybe, cheese and crackers. She understood how artists didn't always take time to eat when they were wrapped up in a project. Maybe Sally would like something more to eat. It was almost lunchtime anyway and Barbara was getting hungry herself. Cheese and crackers should suffice; it would be a light lunch for both of them. She did just meet the woman or she would've offered something more elaborate.

"Yes, that sounds great. I need to get out of here, too. I'm certainly not getting the answers I've been looking for and it's starting to feel like a waste of my time coming here every day." And they both stood up to leave.

Outside Barbara followed Sally. She was a slim woman with a flowing, flowery shear skirt that billowed about her legs, nearly wrapping itself about them and almost tripping her right before it unwrapped itself again, and with hair almost to her waist. Barbara admired the stereotypical artsy getup that Sally had thrown on that morning. She'd never really noticed what Sally wore in church, she'd just noticed her moving from pew to pew. But now she couldn't help but smile at her new friend's sense of freedom and authenticity, not at all concerned about what others may say, not even noticing the people they passed on the way to Sally's car that stared and turned to get another look at the flowing vision that passed them, almost unsure as to what exactly they'd just seen.

Sally pointed to a white Honda Civic hatchback and unlocked Barbara's side as she slipped into her own seat. As to be expected, there were boxes of what looked like paints and blank canvases in the back seat. The smell of oil paints filled the inside of the car and Barbara checked her seat for any fresh paint spills before she sat in the bucket seat.

"No paints are allowed in the front seats so don't worry about that. But if you would feel better, I could put a towel on the seat, I think I might have a clean one back there." Sally started to rummage around looking for the elusive 'clean towel'. Barbara doubted she would find one since that is where the paints and canvases resided.

"I think it's fine. I believe you and I didn't see anything on the seat."

"Ok then. Just give me some directions."

"I'm just a half-mile or so down the road and then take the first right onto Hudson Road. We're, I mean, I'm the fifth house down on the right."

Sally's face changed and turned to look at Barbara, suddenly realizing she didn't know anything about this woman. Here she was rambling on about herself and she hadn't even asked Barbara why she came to the church.

"I'm so sorry, Barbara. I haven't asked you anything about yourself. So, did you lose a husband, or a wife, whichever you might have been married to?"

"Yes, I had a husband and I lost him just three months ago."

"Oh Barbara! I'm so sorry to hear this."

"We can talk about it over tea, ok?" And suddenly Sally was pulling up in front of Barbara's cape with the fenced front yard and a silver Subaru Outback in the driveway.

"So, you don't drive?" Sally looked at the SUV.

"Oh, no, yes, yes, I drive. I just need the exercise and it's a short walk to the church so I choose to walk there. Then I know I'm getting some steps in."

"Ok, that makes sense. Not that it's any of my business." Sally laughed at herself for assuming something about the woman she'd just met.

Getting her steps in wasn't the only reason Barbara walked to the church. Nights were the hardest for her and, in the morning, she just needed to get out of the house where everything she looked at, everything she touched, reminded her of Benjamin. She knew she needed to move to a community with people her age so she could make new friends and learn some new skills. Maybe even get back to her writing on a more regular schedule, like a job. That had always kept her focused. Once the kids were out of the house, she couldn't wait to get back to a full-time job. But now she was thinking of a new career, that of a creative, specifically a poet. She didn't have to work; she was set financially. So why should she go to a nine-to-five job if she didn't have to? She was suddenly feeling inspired by Sally, who worked for herself and obviously loved what she did, creating art pieces. How rewarding that must be! Barbara wondered if she had any skills in that area. She remembered Sally mentioning that she taught. Once they were settled in the house, she made a pot of tea and a plate with sharp cheddar cheese and low-salt Triscuits, she wanted to share some of her thoughts with Sally. She also had to get the conversation off of Benjamin – she'd told Sally as much as she felt comfortable telling a complete stranger about her wonderful, loving husband who'd passed away just a few short months ago. And she added just a bit about the church and her reasons for going without getting into too many details. She wanted to move onto other topics and she wanted to find out more about Sally and her lifestyle. Especially about her teaching. The more she thought about it the more she thought this may be a perfect way for her to express her grief, instead of putting it into words. She was tired of talking about it.

"So, Sally, you mentioned that you teach. Is this a class that I could take, do you think. I mean, is it open to the public? And what medium do you use?"

"Oh, absolutely you could take my class. I teach beginner and advanced. Which are you interested in?" Sally perked up at the mention of her classes.

"Beginner, of course. I dabbled a little many years ago now, but I would like to learn more about it. I've written a lot of poetry but I want a different way to express myself. And I think painting will be a good outlet and a way to express my feelings."

"A lot of people look to the arts, writing or painting, to express grief, if that is what you are thinking."

"Well, to start, but I would like to get to a point of joy, a place of positivity and gratitude. I hope I won't dwell too long on the anger and sadness that seem to be consuming me now. Sometimes I feel like I'll burst if I stay in that place too much longer. But I also know it's a process. It's only been three months, well, almost four now. And all those feelings are still so raw. Still so new. I never felt such sadness in my life, not even when my own parents died. It's different, you know?"

"I wish I could say I do know, but since I was never married, I don't know. But I did come close to it and because I wouldn't give up my art, someone I loved broke it off with me."

"Why would someone ask you to give up your art? That sounds very selfish to me. This is your life, you should be able to do what you want with your life." Barbara was shocked by what Sally'd just revealed about a man she'd nearly married.

"Which is why we broke up. He was moving to Chicago and I was not interested in going there. My heart is in the northeast and I wanted to be close to New York. So, he left. I found him on the internet a few years later. He'd married, has four kids now. Sounds happy but you never know. And I have the life I always wanted. It just wasn't meant to be."

They both sat quietly for a bit, consumed by their own thoughts of lost love. Barbara was aware that they were back on the subject of sadness and wanted to cheer the conversation up a bit.

"So, tell me about art, how you got into it, did you always have the drive to paint? Are you interested in other creative pursuits?"

Sally smiled and checking her watch, got up to go.

"This has been great, Barbara, but I really have to get back to work now. But we'll be in touch, ok? Or I'll see you at church? Ok?"

Barbara continued to sit, wondering what she'd said wrong. Maybe she was getting too personal. But hadn't everything they talked about been personal? She stood and, having walked Sally to her front door, they waved good-bye to each other. Sally seemed like she couldn't get away fast enough. Barbara didn't have a lot of experience with creatives, maybe they were overly sensitive or maybe they just shared too much too fast and then ran from the intimate relationship they were bonding over.

Barbara continued walking to the church, hoping she would see Sally there again. It had been two weeks since Sally had walked out of her house without much more than a wave good-bye. She thought often about their conversation and how easy Sally had been to talk with, and then it just ended. She went over the conversation again and again, trying to figure out the moment when it all went wrong. Maybe Sally had shared more than she planned to and was suddenly uncomfortable, especially since she had just met Barbara. But sometimes those are exactly the people you do share too much with – they don't know you and, unlike family or close friends, they won't judge you. At least she hoped that was how Sally had felt. But they were sharing so much and then they had that moment of reflection and suddenly Sally had to leave. She was sure it had nothing to do with Barbara asking about how she had gotten into art and what other artistic interests she had. That couldn't possibly have been it. She was at a loss and decided she just had to let it go. She was back to square one – she still wanted to take an art class but now she wasn't sure who to take it with and maybe she would run into Sally and it would be uncomfortable for her if she didn't want to talk to Barbara anymore. Barbara thought about her almost new friend and decided that people can be so difficult. Maybe she was better off continuing on her way, as she had been doing, and finally deciding to move into a community with people her age. She heard they had a variety of classes you could take – she was sure she would find an art class and also get back to her writing that she had neglected so long ago.

She was thinking about leaving when she suddenly felt someone sneak up beside her and sit down. It was Sally. Barbara stared at the woman, didn't know what to think, and decided to just wait for her to speak first.

"Hi, Barbara. How have you been?" Barbara couldn't help but notice the pained look on Sally's face and she thought she saw tears forming in the corners of her eyes. She didn't know enough about Sally to judge her harshly so instead, decided to let her explain what had happened that day.

"I'm ok, and how are you, Sally?" Sally pulled a tissue from her pocket and dabbed at a tear. She nodded without speaking, staring at the front of the church as she leaned back on the bench. Barbara could tell she was composing her thoughts.

"I'm fine, you know, I just, I needed some time. But I have to, I need to explain to you."

"Sally, you don't owe me anything, really, so don't..." Sally cut her off and grabbed her hand. Barbara let her continue.

"I do. I owe you an explanation. We were hitting it off fine and then I just disappeared. You must have thought I was some flaky artist and maybe a little bit nuts, too." Barbara smiled at Sally's own description of herself, which was one of the possibilities that had crossed her mind.

"Well, I'm not, really. But I did lie. Not everything. Not about my art and teaching and paying my own way. But I did lie about my fiancé. He was my fiancé, and his name was Joshua. We were very much in love and were going to marry but then he got cancer." She stopped talking and after looking briefly at Barbara looked again at the altar. Each tear slowly ran down Sally's cheeks, as if in slow motion, dragging a line of mascara with them. Sally didn't seem to notice. Barbara reached for her hand and held it tight, feeling her own tears spilling over.

"Oh Sally." That was all she could manage.

"I told a couple of friends the truth but mostly I've told them this lie. Even my family doesn't know. It was just easier. When someone you are in love with dies, everyone is so sad and they really don't want to talk about it. It is too painful. So, I made it easier for everyone and made up this lie that he left me and married and has four kids now. That was just so much easier.

"Except for you."

"Yes, except for me. I could barely get out of your house fast enough because I knew the tears would come and I would be out of control. I so wanted to tell you the truth. Just this once."

"And now you have. How long ago was this, when did he die?"

"Just five months ago. He found out about it almost two years ago. He was five years younger than me so he was in his mid-thirties. We had four and a half glorious years together. He was twenty-nine and I was thirty-four when we met, and then he found out about the cancer. We kept putting off marriage while he was healthy, thinking we had plenty of time. But then we didn't. We both decided we didn't need a piece of paper to confirm the love we both felt for each other. It just didn't seem that important anymore." Sally stopped talking and looked down at their hands. Barbara continued to hold both of her hands, afraid to let go of the young woman who was drowning in her own deep sorrow right before her eyes.

"So, can you forgive me?" Barbara couldn't hold her tears back and letting go of Sally's hands, wrapped her arms about the young woman. Sally let her tears run freely now, sighing with a relief she hadn't felt in a long time.

Just at that moment, a priest came out of the confessional box and, misreading the grief he observed, asked if one of them wanted to come into the confessional. The two women stood up, looked at the priest and then at each other and smiled. Barbara recognized the priest as the one who couldn't find anything more to say than to tell her that it was her husband's time.

"I've got this. I need to go home. And she's in a better place now." Sally smiled up at Barbara and the two walked out of the church, with Barbara's arm still wrapped around the young woman.

Ten Storied Buildings
The Corner Store

Vic loved his little store. He wanted to have his own store ever since he was a kid. The first time his mom brought him to a corner store, he was about seven years old, it was a block away from where his grandmother lived. They lived in the city because that's where his parents worked. There were no corner stores in the city, only big department stores. But when he walked into his grandmother's corner store, it was called "Sid's Variety", the smells of fresh baked cinnamon rolls, hand-made peppermint soaps, and homemade vegetable soups, filled your lungs and you wanted to stay there forever, live there if you could, surrounded by smells that brought the kind of comfort only a cup of hot cocoa can bring. But the store had so much more and everything you might need in a jiffy: butter, lettuce, cheese, bread, milk, scissors, glue, dog food, napkins, tuna fish, and ground beef, plus so much more. It even had his personal favorite, penny candy, in a glass case where he could view it all and pick the pieces he wanted from the many selections. His mom usually bought a couple of items for his grandmother and gave him a nickel. But he had to make his selections before she finished her shopping. The choice was difficult since there were so many that he wanted. But he had his favorites and usually went with them, in particular, the candies that he got two pieces for a penny, like mint juleps and cherry blossoms – not his favorite, they were hard candy, but you got three pieces for a penny. Sometimes he bought Turkish Taffy or a Clark candy bar but they cost five cents each and since he preferred quantity, many pieces of penny candy, to one candy bar, he mostly went for the penny candy.

He cherished his fond memories of Sid's so much he knew one day he would have his own corner store. So, after working for one of the big supermarket chains for more than thirty years, he decided to start looking for a location where he could open a store just like the one a short walk away from where his grandmother lived so many years ago. His wife, June, was fine with it. She always just wanted Vic to be happy. She continued on in her job as a grammar school teacher and since both of their kids were grown and had a couple of their own kids who were now teenagers, he knew now was the time for him to fulfill his life-long dream of owning a variety store.

And of course, his store had a penny candy counter. But he couldn't charge a penny for a piece of candy now because inflation had taken hold and prices on even a tiny piece of candy had more than doubled over the years. What used to cost one penny now cost ten or even fifteen cents. He just couldn't afford to sell them for less. But of course, he sold many other items, just like Sid's Variety did so many years ago. His store was "Vic's Variety". He thought it had a nice ring and always thought Sid's Variety was the perfect name for a store that carried such a wide selection of items, something for the whole family or whatever they might need. He even connected with a local woman, Charlene, who baked and would take special orders for birthday cakes. She always had chocolate chip cookies to sell and oatmeal raisin, too. But her cinnamon rolls were the best and Vic was her best customer, savoring the warm rolls as soon as she delivered them. He always had a pot of coffee on for the early morning commuters and he would enjoy a cinnamon roll with his coffee. Sometimes Charlene stayed for a short visit and had a coffee. But she was busiest in the morning, making her deliveries to other local stores although Vic was her best client. And then less than an hour after she left, a couple of the regulars would stop by for their coffee and cinnamon roll, too. In the winter months they gathered around a wood-burning pot-bellied stove set right in the middle of the store. In the summer, Vic put out a couple of tables and chairs on the sidewalk where he and the regulars would trade stories about the kids and grand-kids.

Counting inventory was a daily chore and he looked forward to it mostly because, when a particular item went down, it meant it was selling. Over the few years that he had the store, almost seven years now, he learned what people in the neighborhood wanted and so had to eliminate a few items and add others that were more in demand. Although people often came in looking for cigarettes, he refused to sell them because he knew that his grandfather had died of lung cancer from smoking and he would not contribute to anyone else suffering the way grandpa Joe had suffered. Whenever anyone asked why he didn't carry cigarettes he would share his memories of his grandfather coughing from emphysema for so many years before he got lung cancer and would suggest they chew gum instead. Or try drawing or painting if they just needed something to do with their hands. They would usually just laugh, shake their head, and go somewhere else to buy them, which he knew they would. But he did what he could and felt good about turning smokers away. He always looked towards heaven and would say to the sky, "I tried grandpa Joe." He was sure grandpa Joe would be proud of him. Even though over the years he tried to quit, even smoking a pipe, he just couldn't stick with it and he would always go back to his cigarettes. A pipe just wasn't as convenient where grandpa Joe worked at the main post office in Boston. And everyone around him smoked cigarettes so if you didn't have any, someone close by did. Vic was glad that over the years, more and more people were learning about the deadly addiction and were giving it up. What really upset him was when the teens were buying them since at this point in time, they certainly knew about the dangers. It was right on the package, for Christ's sake!

Vic loved his store and connecting with the neighbors who lived near him. He felt he was serving a purpose, in a small way, and did what he could whenever anyone came in with a special need. He remembered the neighborhood where his grandmother lived and since this neighborhood was similar, in other words, not the wealthiest people with most of them living paycheck to paycheck, he did what he could to help and would extend credit to some who needed a loaf of bread or a can of soup before they got paid. It was just a few people, at first, but then as more people found out, he added a few more. He was very strict about payment because he knew if they didn't pay each week, it would get out of hand and they wouldn't be able to catch up on what they owed. He couldn't afford to be a charity store but also knew people who were lying, especially when he saw them walk by smoking a cigarette. If they can buy cigarettes, they can pay some of the money they owed him. And then he wouldn't extend credit to them anymore. But most of the people were honest and really just didn't make enough money to fulfill their daily needs of having enough to pay rent, plus buy food for their families, especially the single moms. His heart went out to them. June was fine with him occasionally letting payments slip and forgiving a payment or two, but if it seemed to be happening too often, she would remind Vic that he also had bills to pay and he had to cover the store bills with the money he made. They worked out an agreement at the beginning that he would not take any of the money out of their savings or out of the money they both put into for their own household needs. He agreed one-hundred percent.

Still, he wanted to help the needy. He often thought he should have spent the second half of his life in politics where he could possibly make a difference by voting to get the minimum wage increased so that a single mom could actually feed her family. But over the years, as he watched politicians and the lies they told and unkept promises they made, he couldn't align himself with them. He wouldn't be able to sleep at night. He knew he could do more good by helping people locally, even if it was just by donating a loaf of bread or some cans of soup. He often put his 'day old bread' as they used to call it, even though the bread was usually more like a few days old, out for sale at a fraction of the price before it was picked up by his distributor. He knew they would just throw it out and since it wasn't stale or moldy, he would give it away to people in his neighborhood that he knew could not even afford the price of a loaf of bread. Occasionally, he would throw in a can of tuna but that was when June would have to remind him that they also had bills to pay and he needed to pay into the household first before handing out too much to the neighbors. She loved Vic's big heart and would often overlook his generosity but sometimes she had to step in with a subtle reminder.

Vic loved having contests for his customers, too, so that they could win food by frequenting his store and telling others about Vic's Variety. They could win a jar of peanut butter if they guessed the number of jelly beans in a jar. Or they could win a package of hot dogs if they brought in three new customers in a month. He was always looking for new customers and since he knew almost everyone in this neighborhood, no one could pass themselves off as a 'new' customer. But it was fun for him just coming up with new and different contests. Customers came in just to find out what new contest was going on and what they might win. Vic never had so much fun in his old job, that was for sure. It was strictly corporate business. He could teach them a thing or two about attracting and keeping customers. He knew that in the big business world there was no such thing as loyalty; people just followed the sales. He was able to get beyond that and keep his customers through all their hardships. His customers were loyal.

Vic was planning for his seven-year anniversary. He needed to go above and beyond for this one and had been saving to put more money in the pot for his customers to win bigger and better prizes; the prizes, of course, were all from the shelves in his store. He wanted to hide items for people to find without causing too much disruption in the store. Although children were certainly allowed in his store, from having his own children he knew they could cause a lot of chaos if left on their own. Therefore, the contests were geared mostly towards the parents. He did have a couple of outdoor games for the kids to play, too. But the focus was on helping his customers find creative ways to win more food to feed their families. This was always Vic's biggest challenge. He was excited about the upcoming anniversary and shared it with his loyal customers so that they could spread the word and get excited about it, too.

As a reminder, he handed out tickets every time a customer made a purchase.

"Don't forget your ticket. Could be worth a hundred dollars in merchandise." And the happy customer would take the ticket, filling out the back and putting it into a bowl on the counter.

"I can't wait for your anniversary, it's going to be so much fun, Vic."

"Yes, it is. And you could be a lucky winner. We're going to have all kinds of prizes and chances to win so you don't want to miss it."

"Thanks, Vic. You are the best."

The customers knew how to make him smile. He felt so appreciated and valued in his neighborhood. It just kept reinforcing for him that he had made the right choice when he left his corporate job and opened his very own variety store.

His anniversary day was quickly approaching. Although he kept up on local news, there was one bit of news that he had somehow missed. It was a small article in the local paper. No one who came into his store had even mentioned it. But one day, when his wife came home from school, she shared what all the kids in her classes were saying. She was surprised Vic hadn't heard and was concerned what his reaction would be.

"So, Vic, the kids were talking in class today, wondering if I heard the news and what you thought about it."

"What news would that be? I hear so much news in a day, you'll have to be more specific than that."

"I'm sure you do, but not all news touches you as much as this news does."

Now Vic was curious and stopped cleaning up in the store while his wife sipped a cup of tea.

"And what news is that, my dear?"

June hesitated, not wanting to upset Vic but she knew there was no way to avoid it. He would be crushed.

"There's a supermarket coming to town, just a half mile away, or less."

Vic pondered what she said and sat down, sipping his own cup of tea.

"Hmm, interesting. Why do you think it would concern me?"

"Oh Vic, come on. A huge supermarket coming to town, with bigger variety, lower prices, how can you compete with them?"

"I'm not in competition with them. I have my loyal customers. They won't leave me for a big supermarket. I don't care what they are selling and at what price. Will they give their customers credit just because they know them and know that they don't have the money this week, or even next week? Do they know their customers by name? And their kids, and their ages and grades? Do they know or even care that their mother has cancer and are sharing that with the big supermarket employee because they have a close relationship with them and know exactly what kind of ice cream is their mother's favorite? People do business with people. Not with a big name and all the variety they have to sell in their store. Because that is what it is all about in their big stores, selling. That's it. They don't give a damn about the people. And you know I'm right, June."

June saw that Vic, although trying to stay calm, was getting very emotional thinking about losing the store he loved so much. She reached for his hand but he pulled it away and got up, continuing to clean-up the store.

Over the next few weeks, Vic didn't have the energy he once had and although he did have his seven-year anniversary, it wasn't as much fun as he had planned. Everyone seemed to be talking about the new supermarket. Vic drove by the lot where it was being built and couldn't believe, from week to week, how much progress was made. Soon there was a complete building standing as the builders focused on the inside. And then a sign was erected on the road with an announcement that the supermarket was opening in the next month. The Grand Opening would be announced in the local paper – watch for it and coupons with prices off on select items. Free recipe card file for the first one hundred customers. Sign up on line to get weekly coupons off on their favorite items. And on and on it went, sending excitement through the entire community as everyone waited for the new supermarket and opening day.

Vic noticed fewer and fewer of his regular customers were coming to his store. And when they came in, they got what they came in for, and quickly left, without much chit-chat. Vic tried to remain cheerful but he just couldn't fake it. For the first time he felt alone, that his store was no longer part of the community, that he was a relic and on his way out. More than anything else, he was sad. He thought his neighbors loved him and his store and would forever be loyal to him. But they were just using him, taking advantage of his kindness. There was no loyalty from any of them. They couldn't wait for the new store to open.

And then it did.

And just like that, customers no longer came into Vic's Variety Store. Sales dried up completely. And with sales drying up, so did most of his perishable items. Which meant, not only was Vic not making any money but he was also losing money. He tried to continue to stay open by offering really low prices on select items. But he just couldn't compete with the new supermarket. So, after seven years, three months, and seventeen days, Vic's Variety Store closed its doors. He did have people come in, the scavengers, to get the lowest possible price on a few items. But mostly Vic gave canned and other items to his kids and stored a lot for him and June. At that point he was too angry with his former customers to give them a deal on anything. In his mind, they were traitors to his generosity and good will. He also wondered if the big supermarket was extending credit to those customers who just couldn't afford to pay for their groceries week after week. Vic was sure they did not.

On his last day, he and June went out to dinner and they split a bottle of champagne. They talked about Vic's future plans and what his next 'career' would be.

"I'm certainly not ready for retirement. I'm only sixty-three, I feel like I have a few more good years in me. Besides, I'm not interested in taking cruises, I know we talked about this. I might like to do a few cross-country trips, maybe during the summer months when you aren't working. Unless you plan on retiring. But then again, if I get another job, I won't be able to travel, either. I just don't know right now."

"That's ok, Vic, you don't have to know right now. I think you need to take a little time for yourself. You need to decide how you want to spend your golden years. If you want to retire, that's fine. I'm probably going to work just a couple more years, until I'm sixty-two. I've been doing this for almost forty years so I'm getting tired. And I would like to do some traveling. But mostly, I would like to write a book, or two. You know I've been working on a couple of novels and a memoir. I'd like to finish those before I can't see the keyboard anymore."

They both laughed but knew what June said was the truth. They often talked about aging and knew they needed to enjoy more of life, even spending more time with their kids and the few grand-kids that they had before they were all off to college. But they wanted to continue to fulfill their dreams beyond working, too. Vic thought he would have his store until he decided to spend more time reading and going for long walks with June. He joked that this would likely happen when he was nearing ninety. June hoped it would be sooner – spending her time writing and with her husband were her goals in life. Neither of them thought about being a burden to each other. They had discussed that, too, and each decided they didn't want the other to spend the last years of their lives caring for a sick spouse. This conversation always resulted in them both breaking down and crying. Neither imagined leaving the other on their own suffering with a debilitating illness while off on a cruise or some other adventure. They were too much in love with each other to even consider abandonment as an option. And of course, sometimes these things have a way of working themselves out, despite the plans you've made. That was the conclusion they usually came to, 'we'll just have to wait and see'.

In the meantime, June continued to work and for a couple of weeks, Vic busied himself around the house, taking care of small projects and making sure a nice dinner was on the table when June got home. School was just about over for the year and they decided they would take a few weeks to travel to visit their kids and other relatives. After that, they would just 'wait and see'.

They traveled out to Arizona and New Mexico and visited many of the Indian reservations. Seeing the way the true natives were treated gave Vic an idea. He worked out a plan and let his passion take over. And he couldn't wait to get home and act on it. As usual, June was one-hundred percent behind him on his idea. They both could not wait to get home to begin work on it.

Because Vic had bought the store outright, he had a place to display and sell the items they bought from the American Indians on the reservations they visited. The Kachina dolls, the carved sculptures, and amazing turquoise jewelry, along with so many other items, would help the Indians, with their main objective to help build schools, homes, and feed and clothe the neglected tribes of the west. Vic, suddenly, felt a renewed purpose with his life and was sure everything happens for a reason and this was his true calling. June was also so excited about this new venture that she resigned a year early from her teaching job and put her energy full-time into making this store one that they could each be proud of.

After three months of hard work and connecting with many of the native Americans to purchase their items and bring them back east to sell, they opened their new store "June and Vic's American Indian Original Art". Their first weekend brought many of Vic's old customers back, some with tears in their eyes, so happy and excited to see what June and Vic were now doing. The couple had plans to sell online and turned their business into a 501(c)-3, with the majority of the profits going to the reservations. In a short time, they knew they would run out of space at Vic's Variety Store location since they were also selling on the internet through their new website. They both felt like they had found their lives' purpose.

Vic couldn't have been happier with his life and knew, finally, that he was in the right place at the right time. As he explained to June, "You see, my dear, we just had to wait and see."

Ten Storied Buildings
The Library

The library was her sanctuary. She would rather be here than anywhere else. She used to believe that home was supposed to be the place where you felt the safest. But she knew that wasn't true. At least not in her home with three older brothers and an older sister with a baby, and all of them living in the home they all grew up in with their parents. There was always a game of one sport or another in one room where the males of the house bonded, a soap opera or murder mystery entertaining her mom and sister in another room. That left her room, only big enough for a bed and a small bureau, not even room for a closet, as her escape room. Which she would be fine with if it wasn't right next to the soap opera room. She didn't mind it so much until the baby demanded attention. She longed for headphones, begged for them. She knew she needed to buy her own but was reluctant to part with any of her savings that she put towards her goal of having enough for a security deposit and first month's rent for her own apartment.

But she had one small weakness that prohibited her from saving as much as she might have; and that was buying books. The piles in her bedroom took up most of her floor space and leaned, threateningly, always ready to fall with the slightest nudge, onto her limited floor space. Unlike the books she was surrounded by in the library, these were hers and the only thing she loved more than merely being surrounded by books was being surrounded by books that she owned. They were like her family, except quieter.

Her addiction to buying books went beyond the physical books to include e-books, also. If all of her e-books were physical books in her tiny room, no doubt she wouldn't have any room at all.

So, she decided that the library, her library, would be her safe space and pretend that all of these books belonged to her. Of course, not the sports books, which she had no use for at all. But she was ok with everything else, even the Reference section. Walking up and down the aisles as she restocked the shelves with returns, she would run her fingers along the books' spines, glancing up and down the rows and rows in the most admirable way a loving mother could if all of these books were her children. Lovingly, occasionally, taking one off the shelf and flipping open the book, reading a random paragraph or two, she would sigh as she put the book back in its place.

Her least favorite part of working at the library was when people took books home with them. She never wanted any of them to leave her care, knowing that she alone knew the best way to treat them. She was sure many people tossed them on the floor once they brought them to their homes. Or horrors, bent back the top corners of the pages as they were reading, using these dog-earred pages to mark their place in the book. She thought they should charge a fine when people did that, and she knew which ones they were when they returned the books. When she mentioned this to the director of the library, Mrs. Constance Morris, she smiled at Bailey, patted her arm and said, "It's ok dear, I'm just happy people are reading the books. And you know, over time, books do wear out." Bailey definitely did not agree with that. She knew, based on her own library of books, that with loving care, books could last forever. It was the rough handling of books, throwing them on the floor, and even reading in the bathtub, that caused the early demise of so many books that would end up in the 'free books' pile. Bailey herself had to rescue many a book from that pile and gave them the proper care they each deserved.

But she knew who the biggest offenders were and whenever they came in to take out more books, she would remind them of 'her' rules for caring for the books. Usually they just smiled at her, nodding as if to say, you're crazy, lady. But she didn't care since her main concern was for the books.

There was one guy in particular, if she let herself think about it for long, which she didn't, who was kind of cute. He did seem to read a lot of books, though, so that was a plus. But of course, he was one of the offenders, always returning books with pages bent at the top. And it didn't seem to matter to him that inside every book he took out, Bailey stuck a free library bookmark. She would even remind him about the bookmarks. But again, that patronizing smile. And a couple of times even a wink, as if they were sharing some kind of a special secret! The only 'special secret' they had was that Bailey knew he was dog-earring the pages of the books he took out.

"So, where would you like me to put this bookmark so that you can find it when you read this book?" She made it as easy as she possibly could, but still he ignored her advice, coming out with his own witty remark, or so he thought.

"How about where the sun don't shine." And then a smile and that wink. So offensive.

"Doesn't." She responded.

"Excuse me?" He seemed confused by her comment. No surprise to her.

"You said, where the sun don't shine. The word you should have used is 'doesn't'." And she busied herself with some returns.

"I was just kidding around. I know the correct word but I guess you didn't get it. I'll try to be more better with my words next time." She took a breath ready to once again correct him but saw his smile and knew he was just kidding, again.

"So, is everything a joke with you, is that it?" She was reaching her limit with this one. But again, very cute.

"Pretty much. My writing is so serious that I just try to balance it out by having a little fun outside of my room where I spend the majority of my days."

Of course, Bailey perked up when she heard the word 'writing'. So, he is a writer. Her favorite kind of person. How could she not know this or figure it out based on a lot of the books he'd taken out?

Bailey cleared her throat before asking the most obvious next question.

"And what kind of writer might you be? Let me guess, you write humor, or humorous novels." Bailey smiled at her own witty remark.

"No, but that's a good idea. I write more historical non-fiction which means I do a lot of research, which brings me to the library."

"Oh, so you don't have a computer at home? Can't you just look up the information you need on the internet?"

"Call me old fashioned, but I like looking up information from an actual book. And I find many more treasures in the side bars or by just looking in the table of contents or the index than I would if I researched online."

"But you can find indexes in the information you would research online, too, right?"

"For someone who works at the library, it sounds like you are talking yourself out of a job. Imagine if I took your advice and just stayed home and did all my research online. What would you do all day?" The man gave her an even bigger smile. Bailey felt her face warming up but she smiled, also.

"Well, we do get busy here sometimes. We do have other patrons besides just you Mr…" She looked at his library card to find his name.

"Wilkins, Roger" pointing out his name on the card.

"Mr. Wilkins."

"Please, call me Roger. And you are…" He looked for a name plate on the desk but found her pointing to the name tag on her sweater, just left and south of her neckline."

"Bailey?"

"Just Bailey."

"Well, that's not fair. You know my first and last name and I only know your first name."

"That's because I need to know your first and last name and your address in case you decide to keep one of the many books you take out. But there is no need for you to know my last name or address."

"Unless I wanted to take you out."

Bailey again felt her face warming up and knew she was blushing. She really needed to learn how to control her emotions instead of wearing her heart on her sleeve, as she had been accused of doing. She'd hoped that would come with age. But how long she had to wait, she had no idea. The man, Roger, waited for her to respond. She checked his books out and handed them to him and turned back to checking other books in, getting them ready to go back to their proper places on the shelves.

"Ok, so that's a 'no.' Sorry to have bothered you and for taking up so much of your time." Roger gathered up his books and turned to leave. Bailey had to do something or he might never come back here. He could just go to another library. She had to stop him.

"I didn't say no."

Roger stopped and turned back to the desk.

"Well, that's just fine. How about Saturday? I work at a job besides working on my book and that is the only night I have off. I hope that works for you?"

Saturday actually was perfect for Bailey because she only worked at the library from nine until noon when it closed until Monday. That would give her plenty of time to get ready for their date. But she had to know what to wear and what they would be doing.

"What should I wear? Are we going to dinner or just going for a walk or to see a movie? I don't go on a lot of dates."

"Dinner is what I had planned. Do you like Applebee's? I hope you do. That is where I work a couple of days a week, so I get a discount."

"I do like Applebee's. So, what time will you pick me up?"

"I suppose that depends on whether or not you give me your last name and address or whether I have to do some research to try to find that information on my own." Again, Bailey smiled but turned away from him so he couldn't see how much he was entertaining her. She didn't want it to be too easy for him. She thought guys should work for your affection, at the beginning anyway. She wanted him to know that she was a prize and you aren't given prizes for nothing. He had to work for it. She wasn't sure where she got all these ideas from or whether or not they would even work since she hadn't had much experience with dating, but she would try this approach. If it didn't work, she could always try something else.

Bailey quickly wrote down her address and handed it to Roger.

"Last name?"

"I'll spell it for you. C-u-r-m-u-d-g-e-"

At that point Roger stopped writing and looked up from the paper, smiling.

"I see you also have a sense of humor. That's good to know." Bailey smiled back and taking the paper and pen from Roger, wrote down her last name, and also her phone number.

"You didn't ask for my number but I thought you should have it, in case you are late or something."

"Not a chance. I'll see you at 7pm on Saturday, Ms. DeMarin." And with that, Roger left the library.

Bailey couldn't stop smiling and even when Mrs. Morris asked her if she was ok, she continued to smile and nodded, afraid she would blurt out what she was so happy about if she answered. And for now, she wanted to keep this to herself. Just in case things didn't go well. But she had a feeling about this man. At just twenty-three years old, she really hadn't had a lot of experience with men. This was her own fault because she certainly had been asked out many times but she just didn't find the men attractive and thought of them more as jocks or men who had no real goals or dreams. She wanted a man who had ambition. You would think, working at the library, that there would be plenty to choose from, men who actually read. But most of the men who came to the library and read books were old enough to be her grandfather. And although she might have a stimulating conversation with them, she was looking for more. And it wasn't a father or a grandfather figure. She was looking for a peer, someone her own age who shared similar likes, besides books and reading; but those were an absolute must. Maybe sharing an interest in particular kinds of music. Someone who loved animals as much as she did and also nature, like walking in the woods, not sitting on the sofa all weekend watching football games. She hoped the person she found to spend her life with didn't even like sports, especially not football. She never saw herself sitting next to a man she was married to and watching, all day long, football games. And some guys didn't even care if it was a professional game or a college game, it was just football. Not for her, never. Especially since she grew up listening to these games for as long as she could remember, with the whooping and hollering and carrying on for hours, even long after the games were over. She hoped Roger wasn't that guy.

Saturday couldn't get here fast enough. Bailey was responsible for closing up the library on Saturdays. She didn't have to return until Tuesday, when she came in for the late shift, working from 11am until they closed at 7pm. At least she wasn't alone on Saturdays, which were often very busy. Joey, a high school senior, was usually waiting at the doors when she showed up at 9am. He only worked a couple of days a week, but she was always grateful he was there on Saturdays. He was a burly sort, like an offensive lineman on the football team, but he didn't play at all, despite the coach's pleading for him to join the team. He was a reader and wrote poetry, some of which he shared with Bailey. A sensitive guy, she knew he would be relentlessly teased if he shared this passion with his male friends. He felt more comfortable around Bailey and she knew she could depend on him every Saturday.

When Saturday finally arrived, Bailey found it difficult to concentrate. Joey came up to the front desk where Bailey was checking in returns and looked at her, waiting for her to look back at him.

"Joey, hi, what's up?"

"You."

"What do you mean me, I'm just busy."

"No, no, no, there is definitely something going on with you. What is it? You know you can share everything with me." She blushed knowing he was right about that. She knew he wouldn't share anything she said with anyone else. He could keep secrets. Bailey sighed, knowing she couldn't avoid it so she might as well just confide in Joey.

"I have a date. Tonight. And I'm nervous."

"So, what, you want me to chaperone? Make sure the guy is a gentleman? Because you know I won't let anything happen to you."

"Oh, no, I think I'll be fine. But thanks for offering, Joey. I'm nervous because I haven't had a date in a long time. He might want to kiss me. I think he has his own apartment, too. I don't think I should go there though, not on our first date."

"Definitely do not go to his apartment. But again, I could chaperone and then it would be safe for you to go to his apartment because I would be there with you. So, nothing would happen."

Bailey laughed. "You are right there, I'm sure nothing would happen if you were there with me."

Joey laughed, too, and blushed which Bailey found charming in such a brawny guy.

Bailey relaxed thinking that she and Roger would just go out to dinner at Applebee's and then he could take her home. Maybe a good night kiss would be ok. But thinking about her concerns and how Joey reacted confirmed for her that this plan was the right thing to do.

They both finished up work and as Bailey was locking up the library, she turned to Joey who was waiting for her, and thanked him for helping her decide what to do. Her date would be dinner and home and maybe a peck on the cheek.

"Just looking out for my favorite librarian." She could see Joey blush as he ran his fingers through his hair and after waiting for Bailey to get in her car, and making sure that it started because it wasn't always the most reliable vehicle, Joey followed her out of the parking lot and drove off in the opposite direction.

Once Bailey was home, she took a quick shower and picked out what she would wear that night. She had several hours to relax and decided to read and then nap for about a half hour. Before she knew it, it was 6:30 and she dressed and got ready for her date. At 6:50, her phone rang.

"Hello?"

"I was wondering, do I need to meet your parents or is that not necessary since this our first date?"

"Where are you?"

"That does not answer my question. But to answer your question, I'm right in front of your house."

"I'll be right down."

Bailey could not contain her excitement and stopped half-way down the stairs. She decided that appearing not in a big hurry for her date was the best way to hold a young man's interest. She wasn't sure where she'd read this, probably in a fashion magazine, which she rarely looked at, only occasionally flipping through the pages when an article on the cover caught her eye. When you are over-zealous, you could either scare the man off or he could lose interest because his prize, her, was too easy to get. Most men wanted a challenge, she was sure of that. So, aloof it would be.

The doorbell rang and her older brother, Tommy, aka "Tank", answered the door.

"Who are you?" Tank stood with one hand on the door as if ready to slam it in the young man's face, and his other hand on the door jam, blocking entrance into the house.

"Hi, I'm here for Bailey. My name is Roger, Roger Wilkins."

"Why do you want her?" He could be daft and now Bailey knew she had to intervene.

"He's here for me, Tommy. I'll be right down. Let him come in, please." She ran back up the stairs and decided to primp for a few more minutes. Making him wait was one of the ways to know for sure that he was interested in you. If she was always ready, again, too easy. She had to remember the challenge.

After at least ten minutes, she thought it was long enough and walked, slowly, down the stairs and into the living room where Roger was standing, facing Tommy, who was talking, of course, about his favorite football team. Rolling her eyes, Bailey took Roger's hand and walked him toward the door.

"Good night, Tom, nice meeting you." Tommy saluted him, like he was a soldier, and turned back toward the kitchen.

Once outside, Bailey waited on her side of the car for Roger to open her door, which he did promptly, opening it wide for her to sit inside. After closing it, he got in the driver's side and they were off.

Bailey thought small talk was boring so didn't engage. She looked out her window, appearing bored and uninterested. She checked her watch a couple of times and even sighed. She smiled to herself, knowing she was behaving in exactly the way the article said a young woman who thought of herself as the prize for some young man should act. The author of that article would be proud of her.

At the restaurant, again she waited for Roger to open her door. He had started walking toward the restaurant and stopped when he realized Bailey wasn't walking with him. He turned to see her sitting in the car with a quizzical look on his face. He opened her door and she started getting out of the car.

"Are you ok? I was wondering why you didn't get out of the car?"

"Just waiting for you." And she turned and walked towards the restaurant. Again, she waited for him to open the door so she could walk through. And then she checked her watch and sighed. The hostess brought them to a booth and they each sat on their own side.

"Your waitress is Alena and she will be right with you." The hostess gave Roger a wink. Bailey yawned.

Bailey looked around the restaurant, completely ignoring Roger. She acted like she was sitting here alone. A part of her was surprised that young men found women who behaved like this attractive and considered them some kind of special prize. It was starting to feel like a game to her and she wasn't sure if it was the right way to behave. She looked at her watch again, yawned, and finally opened the menu.

"Bailey, is everything ok with you? You are acting a bit odd. Certainly different from how you were in the library."

"Well, you know, we have to be professional in the library. So, I don't know how it is you thought you knew who I was, but this is me."

"It's just that, you were friendly and now you seem like you have to be someplace else and don't want to be here with me, or you're bored. I don't know. But I'm thinking maybe this was a mistake."

This was not the reaction Bailey was expecting and looked at Roger for the first time. He looked so depressed and sad and he had obviously dressed for their date with a nice shirt and even a sports jacket. He was very attractive and Bailey suddenly felt very lucky to be on this date with him. She knew now that he was the prize and she was about to lose him. If she didn't change.

"I'm so sorry. You're right. I read this in a magazine. You see, I haven't been on many dates. I needed some help and this article in the magazine said that I was this prize and you should work to get my attention and should feel lucky to even be with me. But I'm realizing that I'm the lucky one, that I should be grateful for you. You have been so sweet and a gentleman and now I feel terrible." Her voice caught in her throat and she stopped before her voice cracked anymore and she actually started crying. She'd seen Roger's face and when she mentioned the magazine, he'd given her the eye roll. She thought he was going to get up to leave right then. It was as if he had been duped. She knew now that the article she had 'glimpsed' in the woman's magazine was one person's opinion and not how she wanted to behave at all. He reached across the table to take her hand and she gladly gave it to him.

"Wow, well, that is fantastic. On so many levels. I thought maybe this was the real you and yes, this would be our first and last date. And that I would have to find another library and that would have been a really big loss, to me, because I like our library. But most of all, I appreciate your honesty and am wondering, can we start our date now?"

Bailey sighed and after getting a hand squeeze from Roger, let his hand go and picked up the menu.

"I think I'll have the Caesar salad with chicken."

"Good choice." And they both heaved a sigh of relief.

Ten Storied Buildings

The Motel

Millie knew buying this motel was a good idea the first time she'd stayed here. With only ten rooms to tend to, and no stairs to climb – kind of like the set up in that famous movie by Alfred Hitchcock but without the creepy haunted-looking house looming in the background – it not only fascinated her but the location was one that she was sure would bring regular customers; mostly those just looking for a pillow to lay their heads on for one night. It was exactly what she was looking for: no stress, just a payment and then a quick toilet bowl to clean and linens to wash. So, Millie was thrilled when she inquired as to whether the owner would sell, she was positive she saw tears in the old woman's eyes as she nodded her head. Having worked well into her eighties, she was beyond a reasonable retirement age.

"It's been my life", the woman said and a tear did run down her cheek.

Millie misunderstood.

"So, you don't want to sell the motel?"

The woman's eyes widened, disbelief at the idea that she wouldn't consider this opportunity to finally sell her business of forty-eight years.

"Oh, yes, yes, I do."

"Oh, ok. Great. Because I do want to buy it. I've been looking for a small business just like this."

Again, the old woman's eyes widened and she even managed a small smile in the right corner of her thin-lipped mouth. Millie later heard that the woman had gone to live with her daughter who was a widow and had been trying to get her mother to retire for years. They lived just a few towns over and Millie planned to visit her as soon as she was settled. Millie was happy to hear she also had a couple of grandchildren and even a great-grandchild. After having the motel for so many years, it was a happy ending that she was now surrounded by loved ones.

The buying process went smoothly and within two months, Millie owned the motel. To give it a fresh look she changed the name to 'Millie's Motel'. She thought using her own name gave it a homier feel, like a mom-and-pop shop. Since she was a bookkeeper in her previous life, she also updated the check-in process and after purchasing new stationery with her name on it plus changing everything in the motel that had the previous name on it, 'The Roadside Motel', she was ready for business.

The day after she signed the papers making the motel hers, she had her first customers, a very tired-looking man and woman who informed her that they'd missed their exit and were thrilled when they saw her motel in the distance. The man was a talker.

"So, my wife said, just pull off the side of the road so we can nap at least. Even just for an hour or so before a statey shows up. But I knew there was a motel just up ahead. I found you on Google Maps."

"But you were saying that for more than an hour." The wife stood with her elbow on the counter, using her arm with her hand under her chin to keep her head up, eyes closed.

"Well, anyway, I knew you were here. And I knew we would make it. So here we are. And just the one night and we'll be on our way early. But, I do remember another woman, kind of gray, old, looks like she should have retired years ago, I mean, decades ago. And she was ok, not very talkative though, just wanted you in and out of her hair, well, that's how it seemed to me anyway. You know what I'm saying, Miss?"

"Millie. I'm Millie, the new owner. Yes, I know what you are saying. She was due to retire and now this is my place. I ordered a new sign and I'm calling it 'Millie's Motel'."

"Oh, that's just great. A new venture. What fun. I bet you'll love it, meeting lots of different people with lots of different stories. What a great idea."

The man could have talked all night but his wife was falling asleep standing up.

"Just sign here and you are in Room #4. There is a big #4 on the door, fourth door down."

"Great, just great. So, we're on vacation, you know, driving from state to state. See the country before we get too old, you know, or our knees give out. So much to see. Our plan is to visit eight states on this trip. Eight beautiful states, museums, churches, try some different food, you know, the usual. What kind of work did you do before this?

"I think your Mrs. needs to go to bed, Mr., ah, Williams, Sean Williams."

"I think you are right. Thank you so much, oh, check out, we don't have to do anything right, just leave in the morning?"

"Yes, just leave your key in the room, close the door, and I'll take care of the clean-up. And thank you for stopping by. Glad I can be of service to you and Mrs. Williams."

"Oh, ok. Good night now. Come on Marci, let's go to our room." The woman followed along behind the man, barely raising her head. Millie watched as they headed to room #4. Since it was now after 1am, she decided to put the sign out that informed people that if they needed a room for the night, ring the bell and in a few minutes, someone would come to give them a room. She locked the front door and headed off to bed. The one thing she always made sure to do was to check that the light that lit up the motel sign was on so a weary traveler would find her place. She turned it off only during the bright sunlit day hours. But once the sun was going down, the light would come on and stay on until she got up in the morning.

Always a light sleeper, especially when Roger was out of town and often gone for more than a month at a time, Millie woke at around 6:30am and decided to get up and make some coffee. This was her favorite time of day, enjoying that first cup of coffee, the aroma filling the kitchen with what she had to admit was her most favorite smell. It brought back memories of her own parents when she was a child. The smell of coffee always drifted up to her bedroom and she would inhale deeply. Of course, when she was a child, she couldn't stand the taste of it. She had tried again and again and would spit it out. And then one day, with just the right amount of cream, it tasted like heaven and she was hooked.

Most days were the same after she had her breakfast and showered for the day. She went to the rooms that had been used to change the linens and clean up once the travelers left. If there were a few rooms that had been rented and needed cleaning she would wait to shower otherwise she would be smelling of cleaning products for the rest of the day. Once those chores were done and her own living space put in order, she checked the inventory and then put on a load of wash. While the wash was going, she would sometimes take a nap since she had to stay awake at least until 11 or 12pm. Or she would read a book, her favorite non-physical activity. She was also contemplating writing her memoir. She had a lot of stories to share about her life so far and thought about the stories to come now that she had a motel, ushering in a variety of different personalities every night. That would make for great reading and she was excited thinking about the stories she would soon be able to share. There was a Chamber of Commerce in town and she had stopped in to introduce herself, planning to join the group and spread the word that she was the new owner of the local motel. While she was thinking about the idea of writing the 'next great novel', she searched for a notebook that would be perfect for recording notes about the stories she wanted to write.

It was a Thursday and she thought about preparing for the weekend, which was often busy with more people on the road looking for an overnight stay. All of the ten rooms were ready for customers. One thing she did not do was rent by the hour. There were a few times when people asked, but she knew they were just looking for a place to hookup and then they were done. Even though she would have been paid the nightly room rate even if they only wanted it for an hour, she refused to go down that road of being the 'love motel' in town. She wanted to be known as a respectable establishment welcoming families, couples, whether married or not, whatever color they were or religion, didn't matter to her. She just wanted her motel to be known as a clean and welcoming place for weary travelers to stay. She even offered a continental breakfast with the room on weekends since the prices were higher then. She had met and made arrangements with a local baker to deliver donuts, bagels, and assorted pastries. Coffee and tea were always available in the rooms and she always had them available in the small reception area.

The day, as usual, went by quickly. She was slowing down for the night, expecting a customer or two, when a young man walked into the motel. The automatic lights came on around the motel as Millie was just getting ready to make herself a quick dinner.

"Good evening, and how are you tonight?"

The young man looked a bit disheveled and skittish, like a cat that had just knocked over a glass when it jumped up on the counter, running off with its tail high, heading for a couch to hide under. She noticed he came in empty-handed, dressed in a plum-colored t-shirt and blue jeans. Wondering what he might be up to, she stood behind the counter, ready to push an alarm that Roger had installed. Even though it did nothing but make a lot of noise, it was often enough to scare away anyone who wasn't there to rent a room but might be looking to cause trouble. But the young man seemed to anticipate her move and taking a gun from out of the back of his pants, motioned Millie to move away from behind the counter.

"Why don't you join me over here, ma'am." The man pointed to the sofa in the reception area. Although it was close to the front desk, Millie was concerned about missing calls from people looking for a place to stay. But mostly, she wanted to remain close to the phone if something went wrong. She wouldn't let herself think about what could go wrong.

"My name is Millie, what's your name?"

"I'm not here to be your friend so let's just quit pretending like everything is ok. And I think you should turn your 'Rooms Available' light off."

"If I do that, the local police will come to check on me because I never have the light off." The young man seemed to be figuring out what was the best thing to do. Millie could tell he was distressed about something, probably something he did, and wanted to avoid any contact with the police. She also decided not to mention that the police stop in nightly for a cup of coffee with Millie. Maybe she could talk some sense into the boy by then. He couldn't have been more than eighteen years old.

The boy paced, trying to decide what he should do. Millie wanted to help him but wasn't sure how to approach him without him accusing her of trying to be friends again. She decided to try something, which she felt was always better than doing nothing.

"So, what happened? Did you do something?"

"Why do you think I did something? You sound just like my dad, always ready to blame me whenever anything goes wrong." Maybe this wasn't the best approach.

"Well, you are waving around a gun and threatening me so I figure there is some reason for that. I didn't do anything to you so maybe someone else did something to you."

"Now you got it. People always think they know everything, they know what someone is thinking, what is going on in their life. Well, you don't know. You can't even imagine."

"People always tell me I'm a good listener, maybe that's why I decided to buy this motel. People stop in, weary from their travels, and they always have stories to tell. Just want someone to listen to them."

"Well, I'm not those people. I don't have their stories, I have my story. You can't imagine how horrible my story has been."

At this point the boy sat next to Millie on the couch, hanging his head down. She was sure he was crying and felt bad for the boy. She couldn't imagine what had brought this boy to tears and to come into her motel wielding a gun. What was his purpose, what did he hope to accomplish? She knew she had to tread lightly here if she was going to learn anything about the boy and his problem.

"Did someone abuse you? You can tell the police and they will arrest the person who is abusing you."

Suddenly the boy jumped up and spinning around, pointing the gun at Millie, yelled at her.

"That's a lie! Abusers get away with whatever they want. The police don't listen to the kids, they listen to the dad and believe him. The dad just says the kid is lying and the police believe it! There is nothing anyone can do. You just have to take matters into your own hands. And that is what I did. I took care of business and now the police are looking for me. As if the abuse I suffered isn't enough, now they want to throw me in jail!"

The boy was crying again and turned his back on Millie so she couldn't see the pain on his face, or the tension that caused his body to shake. Whether it was from fear or shame, she could not tell. She really wanted to help the boy and needed to learn more about the abuse and what he had done. Somehow, she was sure the gun was involved.

She decided the boy needed to be treated with care, genuine care, no bullshit. She decided to share her story, hoping it would open up a conversation and he would come out and share his story. She prepared herself with what she was going to share, something she had kept to herself for so long she almost completely forgot about it. But the scars were still there, would always be there.

"I know a thing or two about abuse."

The boy turned towards her, listening for the first time.

"It was my husband, my first husband. I'm fortunate that with the help of a couple of friends, I was able to leave him and meet my current husband, a wonderful loving man. It took me a long time to realize that we all deserve good things in our lives. None of us deserve to be abused or mistreated, physically or mentally. We all deserve to be loved and to have someone to love. But at the time, I didn't think I deserved anything good and thought the beatings he gave me were because I just always did the wrong thing, I always did something that made him angry."

The boy sat on the sofa next to Millie, completely interested in what she was saying.

"Do you have kids?"

"No. I wanted them but he damaged me so much I was never able to have any."

The boy turned away, crying more openly now.

"That son of a bitch. Why, why are there people like this? People who are so hateful and can hurt others weaker than themselves without a care? And they get away with it. Again and again."

"I don't know. And I agree, it sucks. When I finally realized I didn't deserve this, with the help of my friends, I left. If I had stayed, I probably would have killed him."

The boy looked back at Millie, surprised at her confession. Then he looked nervous and got up and began pacing again.

"Are you ok?"

He continued to pace. He was stressed about something. Millie feared he might have used the gun.

"No, no, I'm not. I think I killed someone."

"Your dad?"

"Yup, I think I killed him. I just couldn't take it anymore. Every day I was his punching bag and he was, I mean, I just couldn't take it anymore. I just, I didn't know what to do."

"Ok, sit down here with me and we'll figure this out." A little voice inside said, what are you doing? But she knew she had to help this boy. He didn't have anyone else.

He sat next to her, waiting for instructions.

"So, you shot him?"

"Yes, ma'am."

"Did you see blood? Did he fall to the floor and not move? Did you see any indication that he was dead?"

"I shot and then I ran and I came here."

"So, you don't really know if he is dead. He could still be alive."

The boy jumped up again.

"Then I'm in even worse trouble because he'll come after me and kill me himself. That I know for sure."

"So, first we need to find out if he is actually dead. If he isn't then you are ok. I know a couple of cops and they are good guys and I could vouch for you. I'll tell them you are my nephew or something like that, a long-lost relative."

"Why would you do that for me?"

"Remember my story? Because someone once did it for me. And you need help." The boy seemed to let out a big sigh of relief.

"Yes, ma'am, I do."

"Ok, so can we first get that gun put away? Because it is getting late and most nights I get a visit from a couple of cops. If they see you with a gun they will arrest you on the spot. Or worse. Let me talk to them and I'll check to see if they've heard of any disturbances in the area. I'm assuming you are in the area?"

"Yes, ma'am. Well, sort of, maybe a few miles away, but I walked here." Once Millie mentioned that the cops might just show up at any time, he quickly put the gun down and was ready to do whatever Millie suggested.

"Now that was smart. Ok, so how about I get you something to drink, or a sandwich, would you like a sandwich?" The boy looked hungry.

"A sandwich would be appreciated. Thank you."

"I'll just be in the kitchen – you can come in there with me if you don't want to stay out here. Also, if the cops come in, they might wonder what you are doing in here without me."

The boy jumped up and followed Millie into the kitchen. She noticed that he did look at his gun on the coffee table, considering whether or not he should take it with him, but decided against it and left it where it lay.

"Mark. Mark Ellis."

"Excuse me?" Millie was busying herself at the refrigerator but turned toward the boy.

"My name is Mark Ellis."

"Oh, ok. Hi Mark. Nice to meet you. So, I have roast beef with cheese on rye. How does that sound?"

"That sounds great. Thank you." At least someone had taught him manners.

"Sit, please, Mark." Millie pulled out a chair and Mark sat at the table. She quickly put the sandwich together and then put the kettle on for some hot water to make tea.

"I don't have any soda but you can have orange juice, water, or tea."

"Water's fine."

When Millie had poured her tea and Mark was eating his sandwich, she finally felt like she could relax a little. Then the front door bell rang and Mark jumped up from his seat, ready to run.

"Now, relax. I told you the police might show up. Let me go check. You just sit and finish your sandwich. I'll tell them you are a friend and I'm thinking about hiring you so I don't have to stay here alone at night. Which is a very good idea. Especially when Roger is out of town. Anyway, let me do the talking, ok?"

Mark sat back down and continued eating and Millie went out front.

"Hey Millie. How's everything going tonight?"

"Fine, thanks for checking on me, guys. What's new with you? Arrest anyone tonight?" And she gave them a big smile to let them know she was joking but she was interested in knowing whether or not Mark had killed his father.

"No, not tonight. Although we did get a call from a guy we've dealt with before. A real trouble-maker. And we suspect he abuses his boy, teenager. He called with some complaint about the boy again. We did stop in for a bit, just so he would stop calling."

"Yeah, so what was he calling you for? Did the boy do something? Was his father ok? Or was he just complaining and he knows you'll listen?" Millie tried to act unconcerned while she straightened out the front desk, preparing for closing down for the night and getting ready for bed. Then she noticed the gun on the table and hoped they hadn't seen it.

"Have any coffee, Millie?" Kevin, the older cop, was looking at the area where Millie kept the Keurig maker and her coffee selections but they preferred the kind she made in a coffee pot.

"No, just the Keurig. Anyway, I was just about to lock the door. It's been a long day."

"When is Roger due home?" Kevin was the chatty one and had met Millie her first week there. Dennis was younger and new to the beat. Their regular patrol was from 10pm to 6am so at midnight, they were just getting started and interested in chatting. Millie stole a look at the gun again. She kind of wished that Mark had brought it into the kitchen with him.

"Any day this week. Yeah, I talked to him earlier and he's a few hundred miles away. It will be good to have him home – he's been gone for almost a month. That's usually the longest he's away. I'm hoping he'll retire soon and help run this place with me. But also, just take it easy, too. He'll work on some projects around the place. He likes that sort of thing. And he can't sit still for long." Millie stretched and yawned, hoping the two would take the hint.

"Well, glad everything is ok, Millie. We'll check in on you tomorrow. Maybe you can have some coffee ready for us? We'd much appreciate it. I guess we'll write up that report on that codger, Beau Ellis. He's a piece of work. Mean son-of-a-bitch. Wouldn't blame him if his kid took a shot at him. And he would deserve it, too." Millie perked up and looked at the gun again. At that moment, Kevin and Dennis both pulled out their guns and waved Millie back away from the kitchen, where she stood blocking the door.

"What are you doing? I have everything under control. I've been talking to the boy, I mean, Mark. I gave him something to eat. I'm thinking of giving him a job so there is no need to do this. He hasn't committed a crime."

"According to his dad, he shot at him and grazed his shoulder. Crying like a baby. But still, you can't go around shooting people. We have to take him in."

"Do you know what this boy, Mark, has been through? Probably not. He has bruises on him and it is all from his dad." Millie didn't know if Mark had bruises but she imagined that he did, especially when you were beaten with a belt. That she knew for a fact.

"You cannot take him in. I beg you."

"Why are you standing up for him? Do you even know him?" Kevin lowered his gun.

"I know about people like him because I was one of them. You can't lock him up. He is in my custody. I will take full responsibility for him now."

"I don't know if you can do that, Millie. His dad is still his legal guardian." Dennis put his gun away.

"Well, all I know is, he can't go back to that man. And I can use his help around here so he would earn his keep. He's eighteen, isn't he? Or almost. So, legally, he isn't his dad's responsibility anymore."

"But then he is an adult and would be responsible for shooting at his dad, even if he just nicked him and would be tried as an adult. Which might come with jail time, probably."

"And so, Mark is right. You favor the offender, not the victim. So, what, the victim was in the wrong place at the wrong time? It is just his bad luck? Come on, that can't be true. There has to be better laws than that." Millie was getting upset, fighting not only for Mark but for herself and the abuses she'd dealt with in her first marriage. The laws needed to be changed, that was obvious.

Kevin shook his head, understanding where Millie was coming from since he had seen a lot of child abuse in his many decades as a cop. And he agreed, the laws needed to be changed. And occasionally, he didn't always follow the rules. That was the only way to get around the laws. He believed Millie and thought he could work out a deal with her in the boy's defense.

"Here's what we're gonna do. If you take this boy under your wing, which means, going forward, you will be responsible for his actions. Are you willing to do this?"

Millie nodded. She knew Mark was a good kid and he just needed an adult on his side, for once. Millie wanted that to be her.

"Ok, I hope you know what you're doing. As I was saying, take this boy and be fully responsible for him and his actions, and I'll make sure my report doesn't implicate the boy. We already saw the father before we stopped in here tonight. I saw the gun on the table and figured his boy was here. His father is ok, really just a scratch, but I know it would not be a good scene for the boy if he went home. He's seventeen, almost eighteen, according to his dad, at which time he said he is throwing the boy out. So, just have him lay low for a few months, away from his dad, and when he turns eighteen he can go wherever he wants. Of course, he could take off and just leave the area now, too, especially if he fears running into his dad somewhere. But I don't think the man spends much time getting out of his chair and when he does, it's probably been mostly to beat on his son." At this point Kevin paused, shaking his head, looking away as he thought about the brutality some people inflict on their children.

"What about him?" Millie nodded towards Dennis who sat sipping a cup of Keurig coffee, watching the small TV in the reception area.

"Don't worry about him. He's new and just learning the ropes. He does do everything by the book but I'm teaching him about right and wrong. He's coming along. Anyway, the old man is a big guy and uses his build and his weight to push people around. The less contact I have with him the better. So, I'll make something up, tell him we couldn't find his boy, something. Don't worry about it. You just worry about the kid.

"Mark, his name is Mark. And I will. Take care of him."

"Let's go, Dennis. We'll check on you tomorrow, Millie. Have a good night." Dennis was laughing while watching the Tonight show and jumped up when Kevin called out to him.

"G'night Millie."

"Night Dennis, Kevin. And thank you, Kevin."

Millie locked up behind them and turned out some lights in the office. She always kept the motel sign lit up for late arrivers. It was a system that worked out just fine for her. Although the few times she'd been woken at 3am she'd found it hard to fall back to sleep but people usually stopped driving for the night before then. Sometimes she got the semi-truck drivers stopping in later than others but since that was what Roger drove, she was especially nice to them, understanding the long haul and late hours they put in every day.

Then she took a deep breath and walked into the kitchen. Mark jumped up from his chair when she came in and faced her with hope in his eyes.

"So, it seems there was an accident at your home."

"Millie, I heard the whole conversation. And I don't know how to thank you. No one ever did something like this for me before. Since my mom died, it has been…" Mark had tears in his eyes but wanted to finish what he was saying.

"I just, I won't let you down. I promise. And once I turn eighteen, in two months, if you want to kick me out, I'll go. I'll leave the state. I don't want to be a burden to you. But I can work, I'm strong, I can fix things if you need help with fixing things around here. I will earn my keep."

"Well, that sounds like a good plan, Mark. And I will take you at your word and hold you to it. I am taking a risk by letting you stay with me. I'll contact Roger and let him know. I'm sure he'll be ok with it. He doesn't like leaving me alone when he's sometimes gone for so long. I think this will ease his mind. I never sell out for the night so I'll set you up in one of the rental rooms. And if I do sell out, well, we'll find a place for you to stay in here. How does that sound?"

Mark was smiling from ear to ear.

"That sounds just great!"

"Now, how about a piece of pie?"

Ten Storied Buildings
The Bar

The third stool from the end, farthest back in the room, closest to the bathrooms, was Leo's seat. All the regulars knew this and let him be, even shooing potential sitters from the stool, letting them know that particular stool was taken if Leo hadn't shown up yet or was in the bathroom and would be back shortly. Leo knew this and would give a nod to the others when he showed up and found his stool waiting for him. If the regulars weren't around, which was rare because like Leo, they spent all their free time at Casey's Bar, Casey himself wouldn't let anyone sit there, even removing the stool and putting it back only when he spotted Leo walking in.

"How's it going, Leo." Always the same greeting, not really a question.

"Oh, you know, it's going." Always the same response.

"The usual?"

"That would be just great." And Casey would pour a Bud light draft.

"Having a nice burger and fries with that beer, Leo?"

"Let me take a few sips and think on it awhile."

"Ok." Same questions, same responses, and they both knew what the answer was going to be because it, too, was the same every night. But the back-and-forth banter was all part of the routine they each looked forward to nightly.

If you were a newcomer to town, you wouldn't think anything of it, would ignore the banal conversation most likely. But if you were a regular and heard this conversation over and over again, you might wonder if these two people ever said anything besides the exact words they exchanged each night. Or maybe wonder if you had walked in on a rehearsal for a sitcom. But, it worked for Leo and Casey. And the true regulars, Pet, Charlie, Mike, and BoJo, didn't even notice. They were usually trading work stories, each one as funny as the next.

"Hey Leo, did you hear what happened to BoJo at work today?"

Although the group usually included Leo in their conversations, Leo still preferred to sit on his stool at the bar while the others sat around a table. He and Casey would exchange a few other pleasantries but Leo mostly enjoyed his own company. Or rather, the quiet it afforded him, especially when he had an unusually busy day at his garage. Leo was a master mechanic, choosing to learn, at a young age, everything he could about the Mercedes Benz, the Ferrari, the BMW, and the Porsche. The Porsche was his personal favorite and he would never turn down a job to work on one. He was so impressed by the inner workings of the beast. Over the years he'd found a couple for his own collection, but they needed some work. As usual, the cobbler's kids have no shoes. He was so busy fixing other people's cars that he rarely had the time to work on his own.

But if there was joy in life, that was it. He didn't give a lot of time to much else, except escaping to Casey's almost every night. He avoided home now as much as possible. His girlfriend of seven years wanted to marry. But Leo had already gone down the path of wedded bliss, and that path had been rocky and uneven and full of dead roses with thorns. They'd had no children, which is why it was difficult living with Sandy and her twenty-two-year-old deadbeat son, Jasper. Each week she gave most of her insignificant paycheck to the lazy bastard, which always caused an argument between her and Leo. She even approached Leo a couple of times for cash to help Jasper buy a used car. But of course, it wasn't just any used car, it had to be a sporty car and this one was a Mazda Miata. And of course it couldn't be too old, he needed it to get to the job he didn't yet have. And Leo couldn't even imagine who would hire a lazy good-for-nothing with no marketable skills. He knew the kid was lying; maybe his mom bought it but Leo certainly did not. And so, the arguments continued. And Leo found what he needed right here at Casey's. Peace and quiet with the sounds of billiard balls cracking and a lot of laughing. Occasionally someone would fall and then Casey shut them off. If any fights broke out, the brawlers were thrown out. Casey kept a respectable establishment. And the food was ok. He didn't have a lot on his menu but enough so Leo felt like he was eating a variety. He wasn't a big eater anyway. A burger and fries were good enough for him most nights.

Sometimes when Leo sat at the bar, all the sounds around him just disappeared and he would get lost in his own thoughts. It was exactly like this when he worked on one of the foreign cars. He felt like he became part of the vehicle, which is probably why he was so good and highly respected for the work he did. People came from out of state to have him work on their precious foreign sports cars. He loved it though because then he got to drive these amazing works of art and it was all part of 'working on the car'. No one suspected he was taking it for a joy ride, once the vehicle was fixed, of course. That was one of the perks.

Other than his job and coming to Casey's most nights, he really didn't have anything else in his life. Most times that felt like enough. Other times he thought about what he might be missing and would ask himself, is this all there is? Or thinking about the line from the Jack Nicholson movie "As Good as it Gets", he'd wonder, "Is this as good as it gets?" He thought about this when he was in the doctor's office just last week. A growth appeared on his ear and he thought it was probably from working outside on the cars for so many years and all that sun exposure. But he had been doing that for years and nothing ever came of it. But this was hurting, and looked discolored so he had it checked out. He was just waiting on the biopsy results now.

The bar burst into laughter; it was the guys at the table closest to Leo, the other regulars. Sometimes he was interested in what they were saying and would turn towards them on his stool. Other times he kept his back to them and they would occasionally throw a comment his way. He usually responded by turning his head and giving a one-or-two-word answer to whatever question they had asked. But mostly he was lost in his own thoughts. Sometimes he thought about a vehicle he was working on, figuring out a fix for what the owner said was broken. Sometimes the problem was, simply, the owner. Although he was known to be fair in what he charged for his expertise, sometimes he charged more than was necessary for a job mostly because the owner was such a stuck-up shit, throwing the fact that he was a doctor or a lawyer or some financial wizard in Leo's face so that Leo felt justified in charging him an exorbitant price for the fix, even if it was simple. He knew, even if the guy was sure Leo was stiffing him, that the owner of the vehicle was such a prick that he would never question the price Leo charged him. And because of that, Leo easily tolerated the petty insults the car owner threw at him. It was a trade-off.

At other times Leo's thoughts wandered into the past and he would settle, again and again, on his marriage wondering how something that started out so beautiful and full of future plans could turn a complete one-eighty and end up down the path of destruction. He had been in love and thought it was a forever kind of love. But his wife had other ideas and drove their marriage so deep into the ground it was like she was digging a grave. Except this grave was for Leo only.

They started out like most other newly married couples; lots of sex, lots of I Love Yous, lots of plans of their future together. That lasted for about two years, maybe a little less. Then Katie started to change. Or maybe they both did but Leo knew he was still very much in love. She started staying late at work; she was a secretary at a law firm. So, sure, he could understand if they were working on a case and she needed to help out. But it was every night and sometimes she didn't come home at all, telling him that her boss, one of the owners in the firm, had to be in court the next day so they had to be one-hundred percent ready for their day in court. Again, he bought it. More than once. She started showing up early in the morning, taking just enough time to shower, change, and she was off again, planting a quick kiss on his cheek, running off with a change of clothes in an overnight bag.

"Why do you need a change of clothes?" By this time Leo started feeling like he was just a bit too naïve and Katie had something going on with her boss, and it wasn't work. He tried to keep his cool, not wanting to upset her in case he was wrong.

"Oh Leo, why do I have to explain everything to you? I know you don't understand about law and how important it is, but I can't possibly wear the same clothes I wear to work in court. I can be a little more casual at work but I have to be more professional, wearing a suit, in court. You don't want me to look like my boss's girlfriend, do you?" And with that she laughed.

"I guess I didn't realize you went to court with your boss." Innocent in his reply, he didn't expect the laugh he got in his face.

"You really are naïve. This is a high-powered professional business and we all, every one of us, have to appear professional. And of course, I go to court with him. He consults with me when he needs to make his case and I have the papers he needs. Philip is one of the most sought-after lawyers around. But I guess you wouldn't know that." And she would smile in a derogatory way, as if to say, 'poor, stupid Leo.' Which would cause his blood pressure to rise. It didn't take long before Leo knew this marriage was over. She had no time for Leo anymore. She was married to her job. But Leo had to give it one more try and one day decided to surprise her with a bouquet of red roses and taking her out to lunch. She just needed a reminder of the love they once felt for each other.

Leo walked off the elevator and before he even reached the receptionist, saw Katie in her boss's office. She was sitting on the edge of his desk, leaning towards him, her full bosom prominent in her low-cut sweater. Her boss reached up, brushing his hand across the side of her chest and reached in to caress her breast. Then he pretended to be reaching for a paper she was handing him. She got up and walked towards his window, pulling the blinds down. She turned back to her boss but not before she saw Leo, standing with the roses he'd brought for her, dressed in his best chinos, blue plaid cotton shirt, and the only sports jacket he owned with an expression that could only be described as a deep sadness mixed with disbelief.

She never re-opened the blinds, never opened the door to call out to him, never even acknowledged that he was there. He took the roses, dumped them in the closest trash bucket, and left.

He went home, packed up whatever was worth anything to him, and checked into a local motel. He filed for divorce the next day and, of course, she gave her full consent, wanting nothing from him or what they had bought together while making a home for themselves. He appeared in court, she did not, and it was ruled uncontested. And that was the end. He did hear later that she'd moved in with her lawyer boss and that they were getting married. He also heard that they were having a baby not long after. She'd told Leo that she didn't want kids. He guessed that meant she didn't want to have kids with Leo. But he never heard from her again. That was over thirty years ago.

And now Leo had something else to waste his time thinking about even though he knew it was not the best idea; he was better off thinking about the cars he was working on. But he just couldn't stop thinking about the results of the biopsy.

After a usual night at Casey's Bar, Leo got ready for bed. It was quiet, everyone else was probably asleep. Leo had stayed for one last beer and closed up with Casey; he was often the last to leave. At least he was sure that when he got home, it would be quiet and no one would bother him or ask for money. He was left alone to his own thoughts. He checked the kitchen table for any notes that might have been left for him, sometimes a customer called to ask about their vehicle or called to schedule an appointment. He decided he didn't want to miss a call for a potential job so had the same number for his garage as well as for home. That worked out just fine for him, even though Sandy wanted a separate phone for the house.

"I'm waiting for a call from my sister but sometimes someone calls about their car and I don't want to talk to them. But if you had a separate phone number for the house, problem would be solved." Since Leo paid for everything in the house, Sandy's money was reserved for her and her son, he decided one phone for his garage and the house worked out fine for him. If Sandy didn't like it, she could get her own damn phone.

"How can you be so selfish? I cook for you, and clean, and this is the thanks I get?" Cooking and cleaning was stretching the truth just a little since whenever she made this statement there was often dirty dishes in the sink that she and Jasper had used. And cooking? Mostly, again, she cooked for her and Jasper. Leo decided she should be having this conversation with Jasper. Leo played it safe and didn't reply by pointing out the obvious and getting into an even bigger fight. He was sure that was her goal. She was one of those people who thrived on arguing and believed that the one who yelled the loudest won the argument. After a long day at work, Leo just didn't have the energy.

The note lay on the table, along with dirty dishes that hadn't made it to the sink. He almost didn't see it, except there was a big LEO written on it. He wondered what she had to say in a note that she didn't prefer to yell at him. He opened the folded paper and read "call your doctor".

So, whatever was wrong with Leo his doctor needed to talk to him, he couldn't tell someone else or maybe he didn't want to leave a message on the phone. Or maybe it was his secretary who'd left the message. Either way, he had to call to find out the news about the biopsy. He was sure he wouldn't sleep at all that night, but he curled up on the couch and fell asleep immediately.

The next morning, he was awoken by the sound of dishes clashing in the sink, water running, and voices arguing.

"I'm hungry."

"Have some cereal."

"I don't want cereal."

"Why don't you do the dishes and I'll make you some oatmeal."

"That's cereal, I don't want cereal."

"No, oatmeal is cooked. I'll cook some for you. It's good for you."

"I don't want cereal!" Jasper's voice got louder, emphasizing his dislike for cereal.

"Well, I have to finish getting ready for work. Why don't you wash these dishes. They are your dirty dishes, too."

"I'm busy today. You know, you aren't the only one who is busy."

"Oh really, what do you have to do, why are you so busy?"

"I'm looking for a job."

"It looks to me like you're playing games on that damn phone."

Leo had heard this conversation so many times before, he decided it was time to end it before Sandy and Jasper both started yelling. He walked through the kitchen and upstairs to the bathroom.

"Aren't you going to say good morning?" Sandy watched Leo walk through the room and up the stairs.

"Morning."

After showering he dressed quickly and drove the half mile to his garage. Lost in his work, he forgot all about the phone call from the doctor. Until almost noon when the phone rang. He had just sat down at his work bench to eat the sandwich he got delivered daily from the local sub shop.

"Leo's Foreign Car Shop."

"Hello Leo, this is Doctor Cole's office calling. We need to make an appointment with you to see Dr. Cole."

"But I just saw him. I thought I was getting a call about the biopsy."

"Yes, this is why I'm calling. I'm so sorry to have to tell you this, but the biopsy came back as melanoma and we need to have you come in for surgery. Can you come in on Thursday?"

"This Thursday? That's just two days away."

"That's right. Come in at 7am and the surgery will take place at about 7:30."

"Oh, I don't know, I'm pretty busy right now."

"Mr. McDonough, this is very serious. You need to come in as soon as possible for surgery."

"I have to think about it." And Leo hung up.

Melanoma. He knew it was the serious kind of skin cancer. He really couldn't think about this right now and got back to eating his lunch. He took a big swig of his diet Coke but wished it was a beer. He wished he was at Casey's right now. He wished he was far away from everything and everyone. He didn't want to think about it but couldn't think about anything else. Melanoma. He put his sandwich down and went back to work on the car. His concentration was focused only on that one word, melanoma. He knew it was life-threatening. He threw the wrench that was in his hand, spilling his Coke. He left his garage and drove to Casey's Bar. He wanted to be numb, not to think anymore.

Casey, of course, was surprised to see Leo and looked up at the clock. It was 1:10pm. Leo was never at the bar until after work, usually around 6 or 7pm. Casey knew something was up and after studying Leo's face for a minute, thought it was best to let him talk first if he felt the need. Not an open book, Casey thought it was unlikely that Leo would talk about anything too personal, but he still wanted him to know he was there.

"How ya doin', Leo? What can I get ya?" He continued to study Leo, hoping to get a sign. But nothing.

"Just a Bud light, Casey. Thanks." Casey poured the beer and placed it on the coaster in front of Leo. He decided to tread lightly and not to push too much, thinking maybe Leo wanted to open up but in his own time.

"Early day today, Leo?"

Leo simply nodded as he took a big swig of the beer. Casey realized this was going to be harder than he thought.

"Can I get you anything to eat?"

Leo shook his head, taking another big swig.

Casey couldn't just leave it there and decided to push, just a little.

"Everything ok at home?" He knew Leo lived with his girlfriend and her good-for-nothing son. Maybe they'd broken up.

Again, Leo nodded. Casey realized then that Leo just wanted to be left alone, and so he did. He waited on a couple of other people who had just come into the bar. After setting them up at a table, he returned to Leo who sat looking into his empty beer mug.

"Want another, Leo?"

Leo nodded.

After Casey placed the beer in front of Leo, he couldn't stand it anymore and had to know what was going on with him. He knew he was a private man, had always kept to himself, didn't say much, but he knew enough about him that this was something different.

"I know you're a private guy, Leo, but something is going on with you. You know, you might feel better if you shared a little."

Leo stared into his beer mug, now half-empty, reached into his pocket and took out his wallet, paid for the beer and, after taking one last swallow, left the bar. Casey, watching the back of the mystery man, shook his head and taking the cash, put it into the register and wiped down the bar.

Leo drove around for a bit, ending up at the lake where he used to put a boat in and fish for a couple of hours on Sunday mornings. He hadn't gone fishing for years now. Nothing much gave him pleasure anymore. Just work, wondering what the next foreign car that drove onto his lot would be. Maybe a gem he hadn't had the pleasure of working on before, like a 1960 Porsche 356 convertible. He'd always wanted to own one, but he would have settled for the opportunity to work on one.

On his way home he stopped by the doctor's office and, after making an appointment for Thursday, picked up a phone for Sandy. Then he drove back to his garage and worked for a few more hours.

He decided to go home for supper and had a decent night with Sandy; her son was out, staying at a friend's house. They watched one of Leo's favorite movies, "Die Hard" and then went to bed, enjoying an intimate evening that they hadn't shared for many months.

On Thursday, Leo kept the Doctor's appointment and after a couple of hours, he sat in the recovery room, still groggy from the anesthesia. They sent him home and told him they would know the results in a week or sooner. He already knew the prognosis and he was sure they knew it, too.

Several days passed and the Doctor's office called – this time it was the doctor himself.

"Leo, I'm not sure how to tell you this and I prefer telling you in person but the news isn't good."

"Let me guess, the cancer has spread."

"I'm so sorry Leo. If you had come in when you first noticed the cells on your ear, we might have been able to keep it from spreading. But we found it has spread to your lymph nodes and the x-ray shows it has also spread to your lungs and we would have to take more x-rays to see beyond that. What would you like to do? We can administer chemo, but I believe it is beyond having much chance of improvement with chemo."

"So, what's the good news, Doc?"

The other end was silent.

"I guess I'll get my house in order."

"That's a very good idea. If there is anything I can do to help, with insurance or any issues along that line, please don't hesitate to contact me."

"Yeah, sure. Thanks Doc."

And they both hung up.

Ten Storied Buildings
The Restaurant

Tony tried to keep his menu fresh every week, always having a daily special, as well as adding new recipes monthly. People seemed to like that and came back again and again to find out what was new. That's also what kept it special for Tony. Otherwise, he would've been bored serving up the same meals day in and day out. And after thirty years, it was a challenge. But it was a challenge he fully embraced. The neighborhood where he opened his restaurant was faithful to him and even brought their grown children who continued the family tradition, with multi-generational families choosing "Tony's Place, Fine Dining, Italian Cuisine". He had even expanded about ten years ago, adding a bakery that his youngest daughter, Francesca, or as she liked to be called, Frannie, ran, doing the majority of the baking herself. Sending her to culinary school definitely paid off. Tony couldn't be any prouder. Of course, his wife, Isa, helped out – she was also a great cook – but preferred baking and spending time with Frannie, helping with wedding cakes and some of the larger orders that came in, particularly during the holidays.

Yes, Tony was so proud of both Frannie and his wife, Isa. What saddened him more than he would ever admit, was that neither of his sons wanted to follow in his footsteps and take over the family business.

"I don't want to cook the rest of my life, dad. This was your choice. This is what you wanted to do, not me. I want to be a lawyer." So, Tony sent Tony Jr., who preferred to be called

Antonio, to law school. And after a year of hard work, he dropped out. He was now living in NYC, doing odd jobs, but mostly wasting his time and getting high. Tony knew what kind of people he was hanging out with. He also knew that his mother sent Tony Jr. money from time to time, which was always cause for an argument between them. He also realized that Tony Jr. was a lazy boy and understood that it was partially his fault for giving him everything when he younger. Tony was just trying to make up for all the lack he'd suffered when he was a child. Little did he realize at the time that giving a child everything, to them, means they never have to work for anything. And so, Tony Jr. expected everything to be handed to him without having to work for it.

Fortunately, his middle child, Riccardo, valued hard work. After spending a year taking a variety of classes, he found his passion was for accounting and got his degree from Bentley. His first year, while trying to find himself, had been tough for Ricky and he nearly got thrown out; too many parties and wasting his dad's money. When Tony had seen his son's grades that first semester, he and Isa decided that was it, he was coming into the family business and he was done with college. He begged for another chance and promised he would buckle down since he decided he wanted to be an accountant and even open his own firm. So, they gave him another chance and he made the dean's list the next semester and, from that time on, every semester, even receiving an award in excellence at his graduation with the highest grades among his peers. Finally, a son Tony and Isa could be proud of.

And this worked out fine for Tony because once a month Ricky came to the restaurant, had a great meal, and did his dad's books not only for the restaurant but for the bakery, too. He was doing what he'd said he would do; he had his own business and had opened a second office, hiring six more accountants, to help grow his business even more.

But, with neither son wanting the restaurant, this meant no heirs to leave his restaurant to, and that saddened Tony more than he would admit. He did consider leaving the restaurant to his daughter, Frannie, but he had been taught that the responsibility of providing for your family rests on the man's shoulders. He didn't want to put that burden on Frannie. Isa disagreed with Tony, she knew how smart her only daughter was and thought Tony really had no other choice. He had considered selling the business, but the thought of selling it to someone who might cut corners and drive the business into the ground after all the energy he had put into over the years, just broke his heart. He'd heard this story from friends before when a much-loved restaurant was sold and within the first year it closed. He just couldn't stand the thought of that happening to his dedicated customers. They'd depended on him all these years and he would not let them down. So, he put these thoughts out of his head and kept busy with his cooking. From time to time, Isa would bring it up again and tell him he needed to sign the restaurant over to Frannie. He would just shake his head, not ready to make that decision, hoping that maybe Tony Jr. would come walking through the door telling his dad he was ready to take over the restaurant and wanted to go to culinary school and learn how to be the best cook around, doing his dad proud. This was a dream Tony relived again and again. It really was his only hope. He knew, deep down, that Frannie was dedicated to the restaurant, but her talent was in baking. She loved this more than anything else about the business. He couldn't take that away from her. And at twenty-eight he just didn't think she could handle all the responsibility of running a restaurant. And who would cook? She had a boyfriend, but Tony didn't know how serious they were. Frannie's boyfriend already had a good job as the manager at a supermarket. He was sure he wouldn't give that up to go into the restaurant business. But he did know food, that was a plus.

Day after day, life was busy. There were times when Tony wished he could take a vacation, just a week, and see more of this beautiful country. His parents had come over from Italy when they were first married and Tony and his younger sister, Maria, were born here. Like Tony, his parents had been busy starting their own business in dry-cleaning. His mother had baked and sold cookies to local stores, so at a young age Tony and Maria were exposed to lots of cooking in their kitchen. Maria started her own bakery and, after too much sampling of the baked goods, had developed diabetes and heart disease and had died just a few years ago at the age of fifty-one. Tony had worked at his dad's dry-cleaning business after school each day, but what he'd really wanted was to spend time with his mother in the kitchen. But their mother had Maria to help her and she was the one that learned about baking. Tony had been so jealous of everything his sister was learning and, because he complained so much and accused his mother of favoring his sister, his mother would often let Tony help her with dinner and that satisfied his need to cook, which he'd found he enjoyed more than baking. This is what had led him to his love of cooking. Of course, his father wanted him to take over the dry-cleaning business, but Tony had no interest in it. That was why a part of Tony understood his sons not wanting to work in the restaurant business. It was a full-time commitment and you mostly gave up your life, or any other kind of life, for it. Before the restaurant even opened each day, he was cooking in the early morning hours, making dough for pizzas and preparing large pots of sauce. Frannie was often in the back working on a wedding cake or making cookies. Fortunately, she didn't have the desire to eat too many of the baked goods like his sister Maria. She was more health conscious. She also often suggested vegetarian dishes for the menu, which Tony did not want to do.

"How is that Italian? Authentic Italian is about the sauce and meatballs, and lasagna."

"Yes," Frannie would argue, "but the sauce is mostly marinara, right? A lot of people ask for marinara, they don't want the meat."

"True, but then they want meatballs on the side, so, there goes your theory." It often got them both laughing but still, Frannie would love the opportunity to create a few vegetarian dishes just to actually prove her theory that there were some customers who would love an authentic Italian vegetarian meal. Frannie's boyfriend, Barry, had even mentioned that Frannie should suggest her dad try a vegetarian dish or two.

"He doesn't have to put it on the regular menu but maybe just as a special. People really are going in that direction more and more. I hope he doesn't put himself out of business by being so stubborn."

"I know, I agree. If I ran the place, I would have as many veggie dishes as meat ones."

"So, why isn't your dad teaching you to take over?"

"He's of that old Italian thinking, the son needs to take over the business, you know. I don't know how to get through to him."

"Maybe you can't but maybe your mom can. Hasn't she been talking about taking a few trips? Sounds like she is ready. And if she is ready, maybe she can talk your dad into at least slowing down and passing the baton to you." Barry always said the right thing, but he didn't know her dad like Frannie did. It would be a fight; her dad was stubborn and she knew that for a fact because she was just like him. She also knew what she wanted and, as the only girl in the family, she often got her way. But still, this was her dad's business, one he had built up over years into the successful restaurant it now was. He wasn't about to drop it all in Frannie's lap. But maybe, just maybe, he could start backing out just a bit. And Barry was right, it could start slow, one trip and when he came back and saw that not only did Frannie not burn the restaurant to the ground but it was actually continuing to thrive. Of course, she knew it would take more than just a week. Maybe if she had a month or two. She would talk to her mom.

The weeks passed. Frannie talked to her mom and she was all for it; she knew Frannie could handle everything. Of course, Isa wouldn't be around and neither would her husband but there were others who worked at the restaurant and in the bakery. She was sure Frannie would be ok. She also was getting tired and wanted to slow down and retire, do some traveling. Isa knew it would be a hard task to get Tony to do the same. His life was the restaurant and had been for years. How do you just take that away from someone? But she knew Tony needed to slow down. He had been complaining about his tired feet after a long day of standing and cooking in the kitchen. And sometimes when he got home at night, he would go right to bed. That just didn't seem normal to Isa. But then he would be up at 4am the next morning. It was easy for her to understand why her boys didn't want to take over the restaurant. And she was concerned about Frannie's life becoming just like Tony's. So, she would talk to Tony but also to Frannie. Since it was easier to approach Frannie about her concerns, she talked to her first.

Frannie was just finishing up a birthday cake that was going to be picked up in the next hour. Isa knew Frannie had been working on it all morning and, as usual, it was coming out beautiful. Her mom stood admiring the fine design work and when Frannie put down the tube of icing to indicate she was done, Isa stepped in before Frannie could run off to her next project.

"Frannie, I need to talk to you for just a few minutes."

"Did you talk to dad already?"

"No, not yet. But I have a couple of concerns before I talk with your father."

"Ok, what's up?"

"I know, Frannie, that you can run the restaurant. We have Mikey and Brendan working there, too, and they know the whole menu. And you have Katie helping in the bakery. But I need you to know exactly what you would be getting yourself into taking over the restaurant."

"Mom, I'm here every day. I see everything. I know how much work it takes. I want the chance to prove myself, to dad."

"Yes, I know you understand what he goes through all day, but you don't…"

"Mom, really, you don't need to worry about…"

"Just let me finish." Isa, who rarely raised her voice, was getting frustrated. Recognizing this, Frannie stopped in her tracks and gave her mom her full attention.

"Sorry, mom, I'm sorry."

"Ok, now, what I want to tell you is what you don't see. You don't see dad at home. You haven't lived at home for more than eight years now. Your dad is always exhausted. Every night. He comes home and immediately falls asleep on the couch or goes right to bed. And then he is up at 4am."

"Ok, I see, but what does that have to do with me?"

"If you want this, that will be your life, too."

"But dad is getting older now so sure, he's slowing down."

"No, you aren't listening to me. This has been your dad's life for so many years. And your dad is only sixty and I hope he has many more years left in him to enjoy his life and maybe a couple of grandkids. And that is the other issue I want to talk to you about. Perhaps you'll marry and have a family? The children will suffer if you are spending all of your time at the restaurant. How can you raise a family that way?"

"You and dad did it, why can't I?"

"Because I was home for many years taking care of all of you."

"You're starting to talk like dad now. And maybe kids aren't in my plans. Maybe I'm doing exactly what I want to do. Maybe I'm more like dad than I am like you."

Isa stood with a sad and surprised look on her face. She felt as if her only daughter had just slapped her.

"Mom, I'm sorry, but you know this is my life. I'm sorry your sons disappointed dad but I'm doing what I love and the restaurant business is what I love. If neither of you can understand that perhaps I need to find a restaurant that will give me what I want." At that moment the bell rang out front and Frannie went out to check on the customer even though Katie was out there to help the customers. Frannie just had to get away. How could her biggest supporter now become the one who was standing in her way of getting what she wanted? Her frustration with how quickly the situation had changed prevented her from letting any tears fall.

After a few minutes Frannie went back to the kitchen and her mom was still standing there. She had made herself a cup of tea and one for Frannie. When Frannie walked in her mom put down her cup and gave her daughter a big hug, which pushed the tears down Frannie's cheeks. They stood there with arms wrapped around each other for a few minutes without speaking.

"I don't want you to leave and it upsets me that you would feel that this is your only choice to get what you want. I just need you to understand everything that is involved in becoming the one in charge of a restaurant and a bakery. That is even more than what your dad had to take care of because the bakery has always been yours and mine."

"I know, but I would give up the bakery and move into the kitchen and become a chef. But it would be even better because I know the bakery, so I could hire someone to run it. And Barry knows food and is ready to join me in the restaurant. He's excited about it."

"Oh, I don't know if your dad would go along with that. Barry isn't part of the family, he's just a boyfriend."

"You know he's more than a boyfriend. We've been together for ten years now, the only reason we haven't married is because I keep telling him to wait, that I'm not ready. I don't need to be married. We love each other, that's all I need."

"Of course, but when you have a restaurant together, whose name goes on all the papers?"

"Mine, of course. And Barry is fine with that. But you know, I think I'm almost ready to take the next steps. I mean we already live together so, getting married isn't such a big deal. I know you would both be happier if we were married and not 'living in sin' as you say." They both laughed at that and Isa nodded her head in agreement.

"Barry and I have talked about all of this. He's excited about getting involved in the restaurant with me. He's ready to leave his job and become part of our family. Everything will work out, mom. We just need to convince dad that the restaurant will survive and go on without him. And that is your job. Ok?"

Isa hugged her daughter again and this time she couldn't hold back her tears.

"You are so grown up and I'm so proud of the woman you have become. And even though I wish my daughter would have a couple of bambinos, I still have hope that one of your brothers will make me a grandmother someday soon."

"Who knows, you may already be a grandmother. When was the last time you talked to Antonio? Has it been a month or two? And I'm sure he doesn't tell you everything. He might have one or even two bambinos out there somewhere." Her mom smiled but sadness filled her eyes. Frannie understood how hard it could be for people to accept the way life changed as they aged. People from her parents' generation would never think about having a baby out of wedlock. But, if they did, it was kept hidden and people didn't talk about it. She tried to accept the old ways of how her parents had been raised, but knew she couldn't change their thinking. Her only hope was that her parents could accept and welcome into their home any grandchildren they had; whether her brothers were married or not, they would still be related.

Frannie knew this was a sensitive subject for both of her parents. Having grandchildren. As the only female child, so much pressure was put on her. She needed to somehow explain to her parents, in a way they could understand, that times had changed and many people today were deciding not to have children. At twenty-eight, almost twenty-nine, she was sure having a child was not in her future. She and Barry had already discussed it and this was their decision. He just wanted to be with Frannie. But, for now, her focus was finding a way to convince her dad that she not only could handle running the restaurant but also had ideas to give the restaurant an updated menu by adding more vegetarian dishes. She knew it would be a challenge since he, like her mother, was thinking about heirs. Male heirs, in particular. She had to depend on her mother to talk to her dad about it and get him thinking more about retiring or at least cutting back on his hours, which would give Frannie the opportunity to step in and prove herself. And as often happens, that opportunity appeared sooner than anyone could have expected.

Tony felt exceptionally tired this Saturday night. A group of six had come in ten minutes before closing. And since he was never one to turn customers away, he went to work preparing their meals. He'd let the other two cooks go home and so he handled preparing the order himself. Even the waitresses had left although his longest employed, Tess, was ready to stay.

"I got this. You go home to be with your family." Tess didn't want to go, but Tony assured her he was fine and could handle a few more meals.

By the time the meals were served and the party had all cleaned their plates, it was an hour and a half past closing time. Isa had called but, when Tony didn't answer, she showed up at the restaurant.

Isa was surprised to see people still in the restaurant and went around to the back service entrance the wait staff used. She found

Tony sitting down, wiping his face with a cloth. He was flushed and sweating, and he couldn't seem to catch his breath.

"Tony, what's wrong? I'm calling an ambulance."

"No, no, no ambulance. Don't be silly. I'm fine." He pulled himself up from the chair but quickly fell to the floor.

"Oh my God! Help!"

One of the customers from the restaurant ran into the kitchen and when he saw Tony on the floor, called 911. Two of the other patrons came in and also asked what they could do to help.

"Call my daughter, Frannie, please." Isa handed the woman her cell phone after hitting Frannie's auto-dial button. Frannie answered immediately.

"Mom, what's wrong? Why are you calling so late?"

"Hello, I'm at your father's restaurant with your mother. I think your dad is having a heart attack."

"I'll be right there!"

Frannie and Barry arrived at the restaurant just as the ambulance was pulling away, lights flashing. Her mom was sitting at the table talking with the woman who had spoken to Frannie.

"Mom." Frannie went to her mom and hugged her.

"What happened? I saw the ambulance leaving. Did dad have a heart attack?" Frannie tried to keep the tears out of her voice. She had to be strong for her mother.

The six customers were still there, standing around now, unsure if they should leave or stay.

"The EMT said he was breathing ok. They gave him oxygen and his heart beat was regular. So, they didn't think he had a heart attack. Maybe a seizure of some kind, or a mild stroke, or something like that. But I have to go to the hospital now, so we should go."

The man who called 911 came forward and gave them the money and the receipt.

"No, please, you helped me. I don't know what I would have done if you weren't here to help." And Isa put the money back in the man's hand.

"No, that isn't necessary, really." He tried to give it back but Isa wouldn't take it.

"Thank you for your help." Frannie shook the man's hand and the party of six left. Frannie and Barry quickly locked up and took Isa out the back to their car and headed for the hospital.

On the drive there, Frannie thought how quickly life changes. One minute, her dad, the patriarch of the family, was in charge and the next minute, just like that, he's heading by ambulance to the hospital. Who knows what kind of care he might need as he recuperates over the weeks and months ahead. Her mom, always strong, will take the best care of him, she was sure of that. But where did that leave the restaurant and the bakery? She was ready to step into her dad's shoes, and hopefully he was ready to let her fill them.

The good news was, he'd suffered a minor stroke and would most likely fully recover. The bad news for her dad was, he would not be able to continue at the pace he had been working. At her mom's request, she waited until her dad came home to discuss the restaurant. Frannie had put a sign out to say they were closed for vacation and would open in a couple of weeks. If her dad wasn't ready to put Frannie in charge in that time frame, she would put another sign out, this time it would talk about cleaning or renovations. She hoped it wouldn't take that long.

The conversation Frannie was waiting to have with her dad came sooner than she expected. The stroke was a wake-up call for him. When Frannie and Barry arrived for dinner on Sunday, just a couple of weeks after his stroke, he was sitting at the dining room table, papers scattered around him.

"Sit, sit, Frannie, Barry, come sit with me."

"What's going on dad?"

Her mom came in from the kitchen.

"Oh, Tony, can't we wait until after dinner for all of this?"

"No, I might change my mind." He looked up at his wife and gave her a wink.

Isa shook her head, knowing that wasn't going to happen. Tony smiled at her and she put her hand on his shoulder.

Frannie was quite sure she knew what was coming and felt the tears forming in her eyes. She held Barry's hand under the table, squeezing it from time to time, assuring herself that he was still there and he supported whatever happened today. Her fingers started to tingle so she relaxed her grip a bit.

"Ok, so here we go. Frannie, my only daughter who I am so proud of, it seems it is your time now. I've been shown from up above – Tony raised his hands and looked up at the ceiling – that my time in the restaurant business is coming to a close." Tony stopped as he felt his throat closing up. He shook his head and using his thumb and index finger pinched the corners of his eyes, stopping the tears from flowing. Her mom took this opportunity to interject her thoughts into the discussion.

"So, it took your dad nearly having a heart attack to come to his senses." Tony reached up and touched her hand that was still on his shoulder.

"I'm signing over the restaurant to you, my dearest daughter. I have faith in you and know I'm doing the right thing for both of us. I'm listening to my maker." Again, he looked up at the ceiling, taking the cross from around his neck and kissing it.

Frannie jumped up from her chair and wrapped her arms around her dad. Her mother joined them and so did Barry.

"Ok, everyone, sit down now and let me finish this paper work."

"Did I hear something about 'paper work'?" At that moment Riccardo walked in from the front hall and, after giving his mom and dad a huge hug, gave Frannie a big bear hug.

"I hear a congratulations and a celebration are in order and that 'Tony's Place' will have a new owner. Does this mean I still get free meals?"

'Will you still do the books in exchange for those free meals?"

"Of course I will."

"Then you get your pick from the menu." They all laughed and settled back into their seats.

"Now, there is one condition." Tony continued. They all looked surprised, wondering what this condition might be.

"Ok, dad, what is it?"

"I want to occasionally make an appearance, maybe have a 'Tony's special' night?' Maybe a couple times a week. You know, I haven't worked it all out."

Isa shook her head. "No, what your dad means is 'once a month'". Again, laughter.

"But I will need some guidance and help at the beginning, this is all going to be new to me. And, of course, I'll have Barry so it won't be too bad, plus all the regular help."

"Barry? How can he help if he's working at his job?"

"Oh, I quit my job. I'm signed up full time to work for Frannie."

"See, he said the right thing, to work for me." Frannie hugged the man she was in love with and they both held each other, so happy for where their lives were going now.

"Wow! That's fantastic! I'm so happy Barry."

"Yes, and he has so many connections in the food industry. It is a perfect match."

"A match made in heaven." And Tony kissed his Isa's hand as they all sat down to the wonderful meal Isa had prepared for them.

Ten Storied Buildings

The Supermarket

She never saw herself working at a place like this. With a Masters in Journalism, she was hired right out of college, hadn't even finished her Masters' thesis, and she was being hotly pursued by the big names in the business; Wall Street Journal, New York Times, The Washington Post and a few other smaller ones that she, of course, would not even bother sending a resume along to and wasting a good stamp. She was into the big guys and that was where she wanted to work. And she did, for twenty-seven years. And then they downsized while at the same time she crossed over into her early fifties. Feeling like she was walking through the office with a bullseye on her back, she was soon kissing her several hundred-thousand-dollar a year salary good-bye. But how could they after she had given them so many good years of her life? Plus, the value she brought to the company was unquestioned, until it was.

In hindsight, she should have seen it coming. It was and always had been the good ole boys' club. Even though she mostly wore pants to the office, hoping the higher-ups wouldn't notice the curves of a woman under her matching jacket, being judged by her sexwas an insult she never thought she would have to endure. She'd won prizes, for God's sake! For the company! Allowing them to creep up into the number one spot in the publishing world.

And so, she really never did see this coming. Why her? Why not Jack Brighton, who spent more time flirting with the pushed-up bra twenty-something secretaries whose panties he was forever trying to get into. Exactly what value did he bring to the table? Boys' club. She knew it. When her boss sat her down, her boss, he couldn't even face her. He had his assistant, one of those pushed-up bra twenty-somethings, sit down with her. The coward. And she had always had the greatest respect for the man. Until she didn't. The reason? She was late with a couple of high-level stories. How often, she wondered was Jack Brighton late with his entry-level stories? She guessed always. He had to be related to her boss somehow, or maybe her boss' boss.

Anyway, not one to make a scene, she did exactly that and after the pushed-up bra told her she would be given a month's salary and they were going to walk her out, forever fearful that she was going to take a shit-load of files full of amazing ideas with her that she could then bring to a competitor, the young woman hadn't even finished her spiel when Vivian stood up and walked down the hall to her boss' office, who, of course, pretended to be on the phone. And when she tried to walk into his office, his god-damned door was locked! She banged on the door, he saw her, fear in his eyes, and then pulled the blinds shut. Her plan was to wait him out – he would eventually have to use the 'boys' room. But that wasn't going to happen. Two guys from security walked up behind and led her back to her office, where she packed up all of her personal stuff. Stuff that had sat on her desk for twenty-seven years. Stuff that at one time had meaning and now just looked like junk cluttering up her desk and drawers. Except the bottle of Scotch, that her boss had given her when they won the Pulitzer for Journalism. What does that tell you? She knew that particular Scotch cost upwards of a thousand dollars. She had been tempted to smash the bottle against her boss' door but she thought she might need this bottle over the coming months, depending on how long it took her to find another job.

It took seven months. Seven fucking months! She interviewed with the other big guys, apparently the boys' club had spread lies about her and her abilities, as if twenty-seven years and her name attached to a Pulitzer (along with several others) hadn't been enough credentials to prove her worth. More fuel for the fire that burned in her chest. Then when the other big guys didn't pan out, she went to the smaller guys, the ones she couldn't even be bothered sending a resume to at the beginning of her career. They all, surprisingly, weren't hiring. More fuel. Hey, maybe this could even be a book. Who knows, she might even get on the New York Times Bestsellers List. Wouldn't that be irony at work?

Her new job, as it turned out, was working at her local supermarket in the bakery department. She learned how to decorate cakes and cookies. She was also taught how to put the pre-made baked goods in the oven, a skill she already had. Although baking wasn't one of the skills she was most proud of, she did know how to turn on an oven and mix a boxed cake, even spread a little frosting from a can on it. Cooking, in general, wasn't where her strengths lie. That, along with wedded bliss and raising a couple of rug rats, had passed her by years ago. Kids were never going to be part of her day-to-day life; but, she'd been in love, once. He'd gotten an offer for his dream job in California, she was never leaving New York. And so, it had ended. She'd heard later that he'd married one of those 'Real Housewives' from San Diego. She wished him well.

And now here she was, smelling like cookies after working an eight-hour shift. Her dog, Solo, named for her favorite hunky movie star, couldn't get enough of her and would walk on her heels, sniffing and licking her legs until she put her clothes in the laundry and showered. Plopping on the couch after a day of mostly standing felt as good as a soak at a spa. After eating a ramen noodle dinner, right out of the pot, enhanced with frozen mixed vegetables and a half dozen medium shrimp, she opened her laptop and drilled down until she found her book, the one that she was sure would win her a Pulitzer, not one to share with anyone else but for her and her alone, exposing the discrimination and misogyny that she had been exposed to at her job. It was about time.

Her nightly routine became her reason for living. Other than this she really had nothing to look forward to. Being at an age where you don't just start a new career, not in the work world, writing was the only thing left. The twenty- and thirty-year-olds were the ones making all the big decisions now, particularly in publishing. Although talking to others she kept in touch with and who were close to her fifties milestone, and who worked in other professional industries, she knew it was true across the board – the Millennials were taking over the world. The humor in this was that they had so little experience compared to Gen X'ers and Baby Boomers, although the Boomers were mostly retiring now. And why wouldn't they? Who would want to put up with a Millennial bossing you around, someone young enough to be your child. It would be embarrassing and humiliating. And you might be tempted to take them over your knee and give them a much-needed whupping. Now there's a law-suit just waiting to happen. She wondered if it ever came to that, not the taking over the knee and spanking but some physical pushing, shoving, and yelling.

But the experience, she wondered about that part of it. Did quality just not matter anymore so that the lack of experience that the Millennials brought to the table wasn't as important as the lower salary the principals of the company could pay them over the more experienced long-timers? She knew she'd been one of the higher-paid employees with twenty-seven years seniority over the kids who'd been applying to replace her. Replace her! How was that even possible? She tried to get these negative thoughts out of her head, they were just blocking what she really wanted to say in her book. Although ageism was definitely a part of her story, she just needed to word it in a way that invoked anger in the reader, not pity. She felt enough of that herself without looking for more from a reader. Her goal was to find the kind of readers, like herself, who were losing the battle against the Millennials and ended up losing their jobs before they were even close to retirement, which meant they had to take jobs like Vivian did, with a big cut in pay and not the least bit challenging. She knew there were other jobs out there where she might have been able to use her creative ideas, but at this point in her life she thought a mindless job that'd at least pay her bills would give her the time and energy she needed to write her book. So, it actually worked out for her.

After spending several hours outlining and taking detailed notes that she could get back to and elaborate on more when she needed to, she went to bed and, together with the physical exhaustion of her job and the mental stimulation of writing, fell off to sleep.

Vivian began to see her supermarket job as a chance to observe the public when they didn't think they were being watched. You can learn a lot about a person when you observe them without being observed back. Their idiosyncrasies, their habits, their watching other people, their ego on view for all to see, is fascinating while at the same time can be a little bit annoying. She also was hopeful that this look at the public would help with her book, would show her a side of people that she wasn't expecting, or hadn't really thought much about before. Everything is a learning experience and she was determined to see her new job in this way. Maybe after her original book was published, she could write a book about her people watching; who are the spendthrifts, who watches their wallets, etc. She'd already noticed that, for both men and women, women tended to stick to their shopping lists, whereas men were more apt to stray and throw in their carts whatever they are craving at the time. That could be a fun project and she could do so much of her research right here in the store that seemed a microcosm of the world out there.

"Vivian! Hey, wake up!"

Vivian suddenly realized she was being called; it was Diane, the other person who worked in the bakery and one of those Millennials she was beginning to dislike intensely.

"What is it, Diane. You don't need to yell, I'm sure that is against store policy."

"Well, I called you three times. Someone wants you to write 'Happy Birthday Sue' on a cake. And since that's your job, not mine, maybe you should deal with them." Diane, who looked like she did more than her share of sampling than was allowed, turned away from Vivian and marched out back to where the frozen bakery items were kept. After shaking her head at the rudeness she had to put up with dealing with uneducated and ignorant people, Vivian turned to the counter to help the person looking for a birthday cake.

"Can I help you?"

The young woman smiling at Vivian had the saddest eyes she had ever seen. Waif-like and wearing clothes a bit too big for her small frame, she nodded and held out a cake that she had taken from the display case.

"Yes, please. Could you write 'Happy Birthday Suzie' on it. Thank you."

Vivian wanted to do the best job she could since this young woman, who couldn't have been more than in her early twenties, seemed so grateful that Vivian was even speaking to her. As if she didn't deserve any attention at all. Vivian didn't want her to leave without finding out a little more about her.

"So, is Suzie your sister?"

"No, no, she is my daughter."

"Your daughter? You can't possibly be old enough to have a child. You look so young." Vivian realized that worked for people in their forties and up, not sure it worked so well for people in their twenties.

"Well, she is only five years old, so…"

"Oh, ok. Well, five is a special age, isn't it? You know like, five, ten, twenty, forty, all those big numbers."

"I suppose. She's sick, though. I don't know if she'll make it to those bigger numbers."

Vivian stopped in the middle of writing 'Birthday' and looked at the young woman who now had tears in her eyes.

"I'm so sorry to hear that. And I'm sorry I'm bringing it up and you are talking about it to a complete stranger. Please forgive me."

"Oh, that's ok. I have to talk about it. Sharing it with people somehow makes me feel better. Maybe because it isn't all just on my shoulders, maybe because I feel like everyone I tell is also helping somehow. So, thank you for listening."

Vivian was holding back her own tears now and finished writing on the cake. She wanted to do something to help this young woman but knew she also shouldn't get involved.

She handed the cake back to the young woman, hesitant, holding it a bit longer until the woman looked up at Vivian and then she let the woman take the cake. She had to say something.

"If you need to talk, I work here most weekdays. I could take a break, too. My name is Vivian."

"Oh, that is so sweet. Thank you so much. My name is Candy, Candace, but everyone has called me Candy since I was a kid. Candace McDonough. But I'll remember how generous you've been and for listening to my story. My mother lives across the country and can't afford to fly here so I'm kind of on my own."

"And your daughter's father?" Vivian knew she was overstepping her bounds but couldn't help herself.

"He doesn't know about Suzie. We were in high school and he moved away to college. He tried to keep in touch with me but I was afraid I would tell him about Suzie and so I just never wrote back to him. He told me he loved me, in every letter he wrote to me. He thought I was dumping him."

"Oh no, you should tell him. If she's five, isn't he finished with college now? He might want to know and could even help with her care. You should get in touch with him."

"I don't know. His parents don't like me. They know about Suzie but never told him. They thought I would force him to marry me and he would not go to college then. But they were wrong and I never told him and have handled it all on my own. I have a wonderful neighbor who helps me with her. I've mostly managed, but every day is a struggle for me. I'm learning about food stamps, I don't want any hand-outs, though. But Suzie needs hospital care and I don't have the money for that. Food and rent are about all I can afford."

Suddenly an alarm went off in Vivian's brain. Vivian knew there were scammers out there and for a minute she thought about the story the young woman was telling her. It sounded too sad to be true. She started recalling the story she'd had just been told and looked for a slip-up or inconsistency in the young woman's story that would tell her it was a trap, that the girl standing before her was just looking for someone to give her money and the entire story was made up. Vivian worked too hard to be sucked into a scam and decided to proceed cautiously.

The young woman remained at the bakery counter, as if waiting for something. Maybe this was a scam after all. Maybe she was waiting for Vivian to offer her some money. Vivian had to end this now. She turned towards the back room in the bakery and realized she had to escape.

"I have to get back to work now, Candy, but it was nice talking to you and good luck with your daughter. I hope it all works out. And Happy Birthday to her."

She turned away from Candy but not before she saw her wiping away a tear. Alligator tears? She was getting really paranoid now. She was new to this, dealing with the citizens in her town. Just regular people. How can you tell when someone's telling the truth or not? Maybe she'd been too removed from the real world by her life in the city, working for corporate. You didn't really trust anyone. Candy started to walk away then turned back to Vivian.

"Ok, thank you for your time, it really helped. Bye now."

Vivian watched the young woman walk away and for just a second felt bad at her own abruptness, dismissing Candy after she'd poured her heart out to Vivian. But, did she? Everyone was suspicious these days. You couldn't trust anyone. People were just out for what they could steal from others, believing themselves to be justified in their deceptions because they were deserving. She'd seen in the news lately stories about thieves who'd been breaking into sports figures homes when they knew the athletes were at away games. They stole their awards, money, whatever wasn't nailed down, that they could sell on the black market. Although Vivian thought the athletes were way overpaid, she didn't think that breaking into their homes, their safe places, and taking what you wanted just because you somehow felt justified in stealing or hey, they won't miss ten grand or whatever trinket they had in a display case, was right. Vivian's first thought was always, why don't you do what the majority of us do and get a job. Instead of stealing from others who earned their money or an award, why not try a little manual labor? It was just easier for them to take what wasn't theirs. And now many of them couldn't be identified because, although there were cameras all over the homes, the robbers were covered completely. And, the word was that the robbers didn't even live in this country. They flew in, stole what they could, and then flew out. No fingerprints. Nothing. Not even the FBI could find them. Not like the old days when criminals could be identified on a security camera or they'd leave something behind that could be used to track them down.

Of course, this was not that kind of a case, but there were so many different kinds of scammers that it was hard to know if you were dealing with a person who really was trying to get through hard times or if they were just making up a story worthy of a Pulitzer in order to steal from honest folks who just wanted to help. Vivian decided to just let this one go.

Over the next few days Vivian went about her daily routine of working during the day and then working on her book at night. She was really getting into it now and the research was keeping her focused and on track. She completely forgot about Candy and 'Suzie', if there even were such persons. And then one day, about two weeks after her first meeting with Candy, she met Suzie.

Vivian spotted the two almost by accident; she was putting the cakes out in the display case when she looked up and saw Candy walking towards her, looking at the shelves and adding a loaf of bread to her cart. And that is when she saw Suzie, curled up in the corner of the shopping cart, flipping through the pages of a book, chattering away to herself. She seemed small for a five-year-old and then it hit Vivian: Candy had been telling the truth. Suzie looked up from her book and, looking right at Vivian, smiled and waved. For just a split-second Vivian tried to decide if she should quickly run into the back since she was embarrassed to face Candy, or stand up, not even mention the first time they'd met, and pretend to be a decent human being. She turned to face them, waving back at the pale, frail child that sat in the corner of the cart. Candy looked to see who Suzie had waved at and when she looked up and saw Vivian, she also gave her a small wave and a big smile. She walked directly to Vivian and almost hugged her, but instead she touched her shoulder in a warm gesture.

"Hi, Vivian. I haven't seen you in weeks. How are you? Were you sick? Or just busy? I'm sorry I'm asking so many questions." And she stopped, her face flushed and she looked down at her feet and then reached out to touch Suzie's head.

"This is Suzie that I told you about. Remember?"

"Of course I remember. Hi, Suzie. What's that book you have there?"

"It's a book about painting."

"That sounds great. Do you like the book?"

"Yes. When I grow up, I want to paint. I don't have any paints now, but my mom is going to buy me some soon, so I can paint beautiful pictures, like flowers, and dogs, and trees, all the things I love."

"You sound like you love nature."

"I do. Mom, sometimes when she isn't working, takes me to the park. I can't run around too much because I get tired, but then she pulls me in a wagon."

Out of the mouths of babes. Vivian realized, after talking for just a few minutes to Suzie, that everything Candy had told her was true.

"Ok, sweetie, I'm sure Vivian has to get back to work now." Candy seemed concerned that Vivian might get in trouble, especially since last time they had talked she'd said she had to get back to work.

"It's ok. I can take my break right now, if you want to talk for a few minutes."

"I would really like that." Candy walked back and put the bread back on the shelf while Vivian took off her apron and, after telling Diane that she was taking her break, they walked to the front of the store together. There were tables outside the store and they sat at one.

Vivian had taken a couple of donuts for them to eat. The day-old donuts were free to employees, and Candy immediately took a piece of hers and gave it to Suzie.

"I could have brought another donut for Suzie, I wasn't sure if you gave her anything like that to eat."

"I don't, usually. I don't give her much sugar at all. I don't know what is wrong with her so I try to keep to a low-sugar food plan, lots of fruits and vegetables mostly."

"Veggies." Suzie seemed to agree.

"I always hear 'everything in moderation' so I want to be sure she gets different vitamins she needs without giving her too much of any one thing."

"You're a good mom."

"I try to be. I don't know." Candy wiped a tear away before it fell. She didn't seem to want any sympathy, maybe because it just made her sadder, so quickly changed the subject.

"I did want to tell you something though."

"Yes, what is it?"

"Scott's home."

"Scott?"

Candy pointed to Suzie who was back to her book and not interested in her mom and her new friend.

Vivian whispered, "Her dad?" Candy nodded.

"Candy you have to tell him about Suzie." Candy just shook her head.

"I can't."

"How did you find out?"

"His mom. She only tells me things to torture me. She loves telling me that Scott is dating someone and she thinks he'll get married to her, a good girl. She puts all the blame for my pregnancy on me."

Vivian couldn't stand women who always blamed women for pregnancy. If it wasn't for men, there wouldn't be any pregnancy. The more Candy told her about Scott's mother, the more she disliked her.

"Well, I gave you my vote. I think you need to tell Scott. Just think, someday Suzie will ask you who her dad is and may even go looking for him. Just imagine when she finds out that you never told him about her. Who will be the bad guy then? Not Scott, her dad. It will be you, her mom."

Candy had a look of surprise on her face. It was obviously something she hadn't thought of before.

"You're right! How did I not think about that part of it. I guess I'm just thinking about taking it one day at a time and not thinking about the future. Only because I don't know what Suzie's future will be like or if she even has a future."

"And that is something we need to take care of, too. We need Suzie in the hospital and have some tests done to find out what is going on with your daughter's health."

"My insurance doesn't cover my daughter, just me. And I don't make enough money."

"I think we can find a way around this. Let me help you. But first, I need you to contact Scott. He needs to know about Suzie."

"His mother won't be happy."

"Fuck his mother!" As soon as she said it, she realized Suzie was sitting right next to her mom and Vivian put her hand over her mouth, shaking her head at her careless outburst.

"Sorry."

"It's ok. But I know what you are saying. I have to do what is right for me."

"Of course you do, and this has nothing to do with his mother. If we were talking about a fifteen-year-old boy, yes, his mom would be involved. But this is a grown man who now has responsibilities and having a child is one of them. I get so tired of young men getting off the hook for something like this. You have to tell him. For your daughter's sake."

"I will. I promise."

Vivian checked her watch and knew she had gone overtime with her break. But she hoped she got through to Candy and would be interested to hear what happened next in the young girl's life. She needed to get care for her daughter as soon as possible, too. And Scott needed to know. She knew she was getting way more involved in something that was none of her business, although Candy did share so much with her so she felt she was involved. She also thought about the timing of this; if she had still been working at her old job, she never would have been around to help this young woman and her ill child. Maybe, just maybe, this was exactly where she was supposed to be. She left the fake world of corporate and entered the real world of people with real life problems. Although the job at the supermarket was less than challenging, she had enough energy at night for doing what she needed to do and that was writing her book, telling her story. It really was a perfect balance between the two. If she had stayed at her old job, she wouldn't have had the energy to come home and write. Of course, there wouldn't have been a reason to write a story if she still had her old job. Her entire reason for writing was exactly because she was let go. 'Let go', such an unusual way of saying you were fired. And completely wrong. Like when you are talking on the phone and someone says, 'I'm going to let you go'. You didn't say you wanted to leave the conversation; they are the ones who want to leave. But they make it sound like they are doing you a favor by being respectful of your time.

But helping people the way she was helping Candy felt so good. She didn't remember ever feeling this good about anything she did at her old job. She did what she was trained to do and she did her job well. No emotions were involved at all. But this, she felt on the verge of crying more than once. This young woman and her story grabbed at her heart strings. It felt like the right thing to do.

The weeks went by and Vivian didn't see Candy in all that time. She hoped everything was going well with Suzie and that she hadn't taken a turn for the worse. Maybe she was too nervous contacting Scott so that was why she didn't show up at the supermarket. Or maybe she came by when Vivian wasn't working. And here is the problem with getting involved with a stranger, you become invested. She tried to just forget about it and hoped for the best for Candy and Suzie. She did her job during the day and worked on her book at night. She was making great progress and was happy with the direction it was going. She spent a few evenings and some weekend days at the library, her safe place. The smell of books and the quiet was so soothing to her. And often, she was there until closing, getting to know the librarian who was working that day and engaging in conversation more than once. Concerned it might have been a distraction to her work, the librarian, Jill, was actually helpful and pulled a couple of books from the shelves that Vivian may have overlooked. And then she found herself taking out more books than she could carry to continue working, spending Sundays scanning the many books she scattered on her kitchen table.

More than a month had passed and one day when Vivian was stocking the display case with the new desserts and cakes, Candy came walking towards her. But this time, her carriage was empty. Vivian's heart sunk and she feared the small, ill girl, Suzie, had died.

She didn't know what to say or do, but Candy saw her and waved so she waved back. Strangely, Candy was smiling. A young man came up behind Candy and put a loaf of bread in the carriage, kissing the top of her head as he did.

"Candy, hi, I was wondering how you've been. I haven't seen you in so long." The young man stood beside Candy and put his arm across her shoulders. Vivian decided not to ask about Suzie and instead let Candy fill her in on the news, which she was hoping would be good news.

"Oh Vivian, I so wanted to visit you but life has been very busy. Oh, I want you to meet Scott. Scott, this is the woman I told you about who helped me. It was her idea that I reach out to you."

Scott walked towards Vivian and without hesitating, gave Vivian a big hug.

"Thank you so much for helping Candy. I will be forever indebted to you. I can't tell you what this means to me."

"That's wonderful. I'm so happy for you both. But…" And Vivian couldn't finish but instead looked in the empty carriage that held only a loaf of bread.

"Oh, of course, Suzie. I was so happy to see you and for you to meet Scott, but I should have mentioned that first. Yes, Suzie is in the hospital. It seems she has a lot of allergies and is going through a series of tests to find out exactly what she's allergic to. I just can't believe it was that simple; although it hasn't been a simple process, with so many tests. But she did have a major allergy to gluten and, of course, every day I had been making her a sandwich. They've found a few other foods that she's allergic to, but they believe most will go away as she grows up."

Vivian let out a sigh of relief and felt tears burning the corners of her eyes. She grabbed Candy and gave her a big bear hug, so happy that everything was working out for her.

"And, tell her our other news." Scott was so excited he grabbed Candy's hand and thrust it out for Vivian to see. On her ring finger a beautiful diamond sparkled, matching the beautiful smiles on both Candy and Scott's faces. He leaned in and kissed Candy on the cheek.

"Oh, yes, we are getting married! And we want you to come. Please, Vivian, because none of this would have happened without your support for me and my Suzie."

"Our Suzie." Scott quickly corrected.

"Yes, our Suzie. Please come. Write down your address for me so we can send you an invitation. We are going to have a small gathering next month, not a big ceremony. That's all we need."

"I think you already have everything you need." And Vivian reached around the two of them and hugged them both.

Ten Storied Buildings
The Strip Joint

Jasmine sat staring at her face in the mirror as she prepared for the nightly show, wondering how exactly things had gone wrong. And the same answer came to her every time. Glenn. Always Glenn. A single mom, a drop out in her senior year due to pregnancy, Jasmine had other plans. And stripping at a night club was not it. She loved reading and planned on going to college and majoring in journalism, working for a newspaper would be ideal. She often interviewed people from her neighborhood and submitted articles to the local paper. Observing the comings and goings of the various business owners in town, Jasmine determined which jobs looked the most interesting and would make good stories for the paper. They were thrilled that someone actually noticed them and would pose proudly if they had a storefront business. Or she took a close up of them to attach to the article. The paper always ran the articles; of course, she was doing someone else's job and she never got paid. But she would put this on her resume when she applied to go to college for journalism. She was sure she would get some kind of points for having real-life experience. She was building a following. The people she interviewed always liked her articles and would tell other business friends about Jasmine if they thought they had a good story to tell. And so, she was never without a new person's business to write about.

But all that was changed now. She could still write the articles, of course, the paper would take them gladly. But she needed to get paid and her articles were not in their budget. So, she had to stop writing them; the whole process of tracking down the person, writing their story, taking photos, rewriting the article, and submitting the article to the paper took too much time. She needed to make money. She had a baby to feed and care for. She was lucky that her mom, Dana, helped take care of her daughter, Sophia, a couple of nights a week, but her mom also had a full-time job and would not spend every night caring for a baby. She committed to two nights, sometimes three if she didn't have plans and didn't mind staying home. Sophia was her grand-daughter, after all. The other two nights Jasmine hired a babysitter. Jasmine knew she had to get her high school diploma first; she'd been about five months away from graduation when Sophia had been born. An online service would allow her to take the GED. Once she received her diploma, she planned on applying to the state college where she also hoped to take classes online. And hopefully, because of her situation, she could get a scholarship to help pay for school. She studied whenever and wherever she could, mostly at home while Sophia was sleeping and sometimes at work while she was waiting to go on stage like now.

Jasmine was fortunate that she still lived with her mom. Even though her mom had given Jasmine condoms and had told her all about the risks involved, condoms didn't always work. But her mom also knew it took two people to make a baby and had refused to put the blame completely on her daughter. Dana had tried talking to Glenn's parents, but they refused to believe that the baby was Glenn's, implying that any number of boys could be the father, just short of calling Jasmine a whore. Dana came so close to sucker-punching Glenn's mom when she said this that Jasmine had to pull her back. Dana had had her fill of always blaming the woman for an unwanted pregnancy. Dana knew Jasmine loved Glenn but wished her daughter could have waited at least until she had finished high school. If she had gone on to college, she thought for sure Glenn would have moved on to the next one, as he had done as soon as Jasmine had told him she was pregnant. But at least now Jasmine knew who Glenn really was and most likely had saved herself from a divorce. Like a lot of young men, Glenn was all about the next conquest. Dana knew this, but it is sometimes difficult explaining something this simple to a young woman who believes herself to be in love. Dana had made the same mistakes when she was Jasmine's age but she never got pregnant. And she was fortunate that she met her knight in shining armor while in college. Little did either of them know that the car accident, caused by a teen who was texting, would take the love of her life from her just ten years into their marriage, leaving a grieving wife and a sweet seven-year-old daughter at home. Fortunately, Dana made a good living so Jasmine had never wanted for anything, except her dad.

But now Dana felt there wasn't much more she could do to help her daughter; these were the lessons Jasmine needed to learn on her own. Jasmine knew her mom loved her and her baby, Sophia, and would give her life for either of them. But she was only in her forties and had her career and her own life, too. She didn't expect her mom to give either up just because she'd met a shit and fell in love. Dana wished Jasmine had met a guy like her dad had been, an upstanding man who cared about and valued women, not one who got what he wanted and then discarded them like trash. She also wished Jasmine would find another job; baring it all was not what she wanted for her daughter. But as Jasmine reasoned, she couldn't make this much money anywhere else with a high school diploma, which she didn't even have, yet.

Her mom was obviously concerned for her welfare when she'd asked, "But what about the grabbers, or guys who think because they've watched you strip and know what your body looks like, that they can now have their way with you."

Jasmine had replied, "One thing the management is adamant about, mom, is protecting their ladies. That would never happen. If they see a troublemaker, he's banned from the club. They also walk us to our cars at night in case some weirdo's stalking us. So, I feel pretty safe."

Jasmine snapped out of her trance when one of the dancers, Dani Dungeon Dragon, which was her stage name, came in to put her makeup and outfit on. Jasmine's stage name was Jazzy Jiggle Jugs, which she hated, blaming it on the fact that she was well-endowed. Unless she could come up with a better name, she was stuck with it. Dani had an excellent figure, she was an aerobics instructor on her nights off, and also worked for her uncle's construction company in the accounting office. Jasmine would love to get a job somewhere else but knew there wasn't an office job around that would pay anything like she made at this job. Her goal, always, was to get her degree. She would keep dancing until she could pay for college, or until she got the scholarship she planned on applying for; hopefully that would happen. She wanted more than anything to be able to enroll before the start of the new semester.

"Hey, Jazzy. How's it goin'?" That was one of the things that Jasmine liked about this job, the other girls were really nice. They all had some story to tell, some guy who screwed them over, or a job that fell through. None of them really wanted to be here and were just waiting for the right job to come their way. Some of them had been here longer than others and it showed; they just put a little more pancake makeup on, hoping that the boss wouldn't notice they were aging and would give them a break, let them hang in there a little bit longer as long as the customers didn't complain. They had to work out a little more, too, to keep their shapes tight and their breasts high. Some even had breast lifts if they were bigger than most; you just couldn't avoid the sagging. Jasmine planned on being out of here long before she had to worry about her body changing that much.

"I'm good. How about you?"

"I'm exhausted! I can't keep juggling three jobs much longer. I might have to tell my uncle I can't do his books anymore."

"Oh, that's too bad. I always think it's great to have a family member who has a business and keeps it in the family, you know."

"Yeah, except this family member is kind of taking advantage of me. He pays me almost nothing, ever since I was in high school and that was five years ago. He never gave me a raise because, you know, I'm 'family'. So, I think I need to give him the boot. I need to make more money now. I don't need charity work. It isn't like he's going to leave the business to me anyway."

"I see what you mean, Dani. That sucks. Maybe you could do the same kind of accounting work but for someone who pays better?"

"I've thought about that. Of course, it's my mom's brother so I'd never hear the end of it. Italians! They love to have something to bitch about. My poor mom, though, she'll be right in the middle of it all. I don't want to do that to her, either. I don't know, I'll figure something out."

"Good luck with that, Dani. I wish I had an answer for you."

"You're sweet, kid." Dani gave Jasmine a kiss on the top of her head.

Several of the other dancers arrived; Kuddly Kitty, Bodacious Brenda, and Sexy Shannon. This was Jasmine's favorite time of working here. Many of the other girls would show up a little early so they could hang out and chat, share love stories - which were usually sad stories - and have some girl time while helping each other with their hair and makeup.

When Jasmine had finished putting on her makeup, she sat at a table at the back of the bar, waiting for her turn on stage. As usual, she brought a notebook and the study guide that she was using to prepare for taking the GED. Sitting at the back of the bar, she was nearly invisible, particularly once the show started and all eyes were on the stage. Except on this particular night, a young man had been watching her from a table on the other side of the room. She noticed him, also, because he didn't really seem to be watching the show but was writing instead, sipping a beer from time to time. As she hoped someday to be a journalist, Jasmine always noticed when someone was writing. One time when she was looking over at him, he looked up and saw her looking at him. She quickly put her head down and continued studying her notes. In a few minutes she felt someone standing over her and looked up to see a good-looking, dark-haired, man looking down at her. It was the man who had been sitting across the room, writing.

"Hi, I'm Jake, Jake Wilcott. Do you mind if I talk to you for a few minutes?" He was very polite, but Jasmine had become suspicious of the polite ones; they were usually looking for something.

"Well, I'm going to go on in a bit, so, I don't know."

"I won't take a lot of your time. I just had a couple of questions."

And now Jasmine was really suspicious. The questions were usually, 'What time do you get off?' and 'Do you date men from the club?'. Some got really crude and asked if she gave blow-jobs. These were usually guys from out-of-town and, after a quick wave to one of the bouncers, were quickly escorted out and told, in a voice loud enough for all to hear, to never come back.

"I've heard them all before and if you ask the wrong ones, just warning you, you will be escorted out of here and not by me." She looked up, searching for Bonkers, who got the nickname because if a guy gave him any trouble, he would go bonkers. And most guys knew enough to do whatever Bonkers said the first time he told them to do it.

"Oh, no worries, I won't ask anything the least bit offensive. May I?" Jake pointed to the other chair at her table and when Jasmine nodded, he sat down.

"I've seen you here before and you always seem to have your head in a book. Are you a student? And, if you are, what are you studying?"

"Well, that is not what I expected." And Jasmine smiled for the first time at the young man.

"I am studying. I'm taking the GED next week."

"Oh, high school! I did not expect that. I thought you were studying for college."

"Sorry to disappoint you." Jasmine's smile faded and she turned back to her book.

"No, no, I'm sorry. I didn't mean anything by that. Let me explain. I'm a reporter, writing about strippers and dancers and the incredible diversity and backgrounds that they all come from. Can you tell me your name and would you be interested in helping me with my article. I write for the Boston Globe."

Jasmine was a little star-struck now. She didn't get excited over meeting a Hollywood star, she was more fascinated by people in the writing industry, authors and journalists in particular.

"Wow, that is fantastic. That is exactly what I am going to go to college for, journalism. That is so exciting. Can I ask you how you got the job and what you studied in college and oh, do you have to know someone in the field to get a job and…" She stopped when she saw Jake smiling at her.

"I'm sorry, I just always wanted to know so many things about this field. I worked, for free of course, for our local paper when I was in high school. I just loved interviewing business people in our town and writing articles about them."

"Do you still do that?"

"No, I had to stop that when I got pregnant and had to drop out of school and get a job. And this is the kind of job you get when you don't have a college or even a high school education."

"So sorry, that must have been hard for you. Do you mind if I take notes?"

"Oh sure, no problem. You've probably heard the story before, girl meets boy, girl falls for boy, girl gets pregnant, and then boy acts like he doesn't know you and wants nothing to do with you ever again."

"What a dick. I'm sorry you went through that. So, you have a child now?"

"Yes, and I have to work to pay for her care and put money towards college."

"Do you have family who can help you out?"

"I live with my mom, but she works and will take my daughter only a couple of nights a week. I appreciate everything she has done to help me with Sophia, um, my daughter. I don't want her name mentioned, please."

"No need to mention it."

"And you have not answered my questions yet."

"How about I answer all your questions over dinner."

"Oh, I don't know. I don't know you and don't know if I should trust you."

"Fair enough. What would you suggest then? I'll leave it completely up to you."

"That's nice, I appreciate that. Well, do you come here often?"

Jake laughed. "Isn't that supposed to be my line?"

Jasmine laughed, too, and blushed a little.

"What I was thinking was on the days I'm working, I can get here a little earlier and we could talk then."

"Ok, that will work for me. If you noticed, I didn't really come here for the show but to get some work done. And, it so happens I am working on this story, as I mentioned, about strippers and dancers. But, I have come here in the past because I seem to be able to get so much more work done."

"So, you don't come here for the show? Oh, I get it, because you're gay so you aren't distracted by the attractive women taking their clothes off and dancing."

"No, I'm not gay. And yes, I do sneak a peek from time to time, but I prefer the mystery of women having a little something on, leaving something to your imagination what is underneath instead of just having it all out there for everyone to see."

"Then an old-fashioned kind of guy."

"Sort of, maybe not that old-fashioned. I can do without the bloomers and lots of layers like they used to wear in the 1800s." Now it was Jake's turn to blush. Jasmine giggled.

One of the managers gestured to Jasmine that she was on next. She nodded and put her books away.

"Sorry, but I have to go now. Also, I don't take all of my clothes off, just enough."

"Ah, yes, I did notice. So, um..."

"Not gay."

"Not gay, right." And again, Jake's face turned pink.

Jasmine quickly wrote her name and home number on a piece of paper and handed it to Jake.

"If you don't see me here, you can call me."

"Thanks, Jasmine."

Jake continued sitting at the table and took some more notes. When Jasmine went on stage, Jake had his head down, writing through her entire act. She did look over at one point and saw him look up and then put his head down, almost as if embarrassed to be caught looking at her. Or maybe he was just thinking about his story and didn't really even see her, but she was pretty sure he did. He was cute, too. She hoped he was single.

Several weeks went by and Jasmine didn't see Jake again. Then on a Friday night he was there, at the same table, writing. She peeked out from the back room and when he saw her, he waved her over.

"Hi Jake, I haven't seen you for a while. How are you?"

"I'm good. So, I have more questions for you. Do you have time?"

"Sorry, not tonight."

"How about tomorrow. I could take you and your daughter out to breakfast or lunch, whatever works for you."

"I don't know how much work you would get done, my daughter is quite the little chatter box."

"Sounds great. I'm sure we can work with her. Does she like coloring? And can you tell me how old she is?"

"She's almost three. And she loves coloring."

"Great, I have access to coloring books for kids and can bring a couple she might like."

"Oh, are they your kid's coloring books?"

"No, my sister's kids. She has two, two girls, and they have more coloring books than they know what to do with. I know I can 'borrow' a couple of them. And I'll snag a box of crayons, too. So, is it a date?"

"Is it a date?"

"You know what I mean, can we get together, breakfast or lunch, you pick."

"Sure, lunch would be good."

"Great. I'll call you and pick you up around noontime. And, if I were taking you out on a date, it would be a proper date, just you and me and out to dinner at a nice restaurant."

"Like an old-fashioned kind of guy."

Jake laughed. "Sort of."

Jasmine couldn't wait for her lunch date with Jake. She hoped Sophia would let them talk, she didn't let her nap after breakfast thinking she might nap while they were talking instead. Or love the coloring books so much she would be completely absorbed by them and go into her own little world, as Jasmine noticed she sometimes did. Either way, she wanted to give Jake enough time to work on his article and also answer some of the questions she had about the world of journalism.

But, he didn't call. And of course, she didn't have any way of getting in touch with him. She went into her 'I hate men' place and sat around the house brooding. Her mom knew something was up and when she told her about Jake she nodded.

"You know, something might have happened. From what you've told me, he sounds like an upstanding guy."

"Mom, I can't believe you are making excuses for him. You, of all people, should know men."

"What do you mean, 'me of all people' – I was married to a wonderful man, remember? Your father? And not right out of high school. I married him when we were both ready. So, yes, there are some great guys around. And I know there are shits, too. But Jake, from what you've told me, doesn't sound like one of those guys. All I'm saying is, see what he has to say."

Jasmine knew her mom was right. She would listen to what Jake had to say and she was sure she would be able to spot a lie if he started telling her one.

Days went by and no Jake. Jasmine told herself that he got what he wanted from her and he was done. He probably finished his article and didn't need her anymore so moved onto his next story. Again, typical men. She wouldn't let her mom tell her otherwise; after what she went through with Glenn, how could she ever trust a man again. And now Jake, talking about them going on a date and taking her and Sophia out to lunch and just nothing, not even a god-damned phone call! What a piece of shit! That was it. She just couldn't take men anymore. She wanted nothing to do with them. Even this job was getting to her, knowing that men were watching her. Men, the enemy, and she was showing her body to them, they didn't deserve to look at her, she was too good for all men. That was it, she was quitting her job. She'd get a low-paying office job, she just didn't care anymore.

Weeks passed. Jasmine gave her notice at work; the only thing she would miss was the camaraderie with the other strippers. She loved having that support – it was like she had a half-dozen big sisters. They all hated to see her go. And then, when another couple of weeks had passed, she got a job at the local newspaper office, answering phones and taking messages. She even got to write up obituaries and some small local news items like when a cat was stuck in a tree. It didn't pay anywhere near what she made stripping, but she was where she wanted to be and her mom said she would help with college. She did get her GED and was just waiting to hear about a scholarship she had applied for. Her mom was proud of her and saw how much she worked for what she wanted. It would just maybe take a bit longer since she could only take a couple of classes each semester. But she was moving forward and that was the most important thing. She just wanted to be a mom Sophia would be proud of and right now, she was proud of herself. That was more important than anything else.

It was a particularly busy Friday. The reporters were in and out, trying to finish up articles before the paper had to go to press. The phones were ringing and many people were showing up looking for reporters to talk to with the waiting room getting more crowded. Jasmine kept her cool, though, and handled everyone with ease, a quality they all appreciated at the paper. She noticed a young man coming in on crutches, people helping him maneuver the crutches and helping him sit in a chair near the back of the busy room. Jasmine didn't think she'd have time to help him but when she had taken care of most of the others in the room, she called out to the man to see to see how she could help him.

"Excuse me, young man, who are you here to see, can I get someone for you?"

"You, I'm here to talk to you."

"Yes, you are talking to me now but I have to set you up with a reporter or an editor, so can you just tell me who you are here to see or should I let someone know you are here?"

Again, the man just said, "You, I'm here to see you."

Jasmine was getting frustrated with the man and was about to walk over to him, remembering that he was on crutches when suddenly he appeared in front of her desk. When she looked up, she recognized Jake immediately.

"I believe I owe you a lunch."

"Oh, my God! Jake, what happened?" She ran around the desk and escorted Jake back to the chair where he had been sitting.

"What the hell, Jake! Crutches, why are you on crutches?"

"So, remember a couple of months ago we had a lunch date? Well, I was on my way over to pick you up and just about to call you when a guy in a truck slammed into the side of my car. Fortunately, he hit the passenger side or, as my doctor said, I probably wouldn't have survived. Anyway, to make a long story short, I've been in the hospital. I've had a couple of surgeries to repair my right leg that was crushed in the accident, and here I am. It took me a long time to get here but I'm ready for that lunch date now, if you'll still go out with me."

"Of course I will. But how did you find me?"

"I called your house and talked to your mom. She gave me your cell number, but I knew if I called you, you'd just hang up."

"I would have!"

"Anyway, she told me you were doing great and got your GED and that you were working here now and waiting to hear about a scholarship you had applied for to help with college. That's fantastic. I wanted to congratulate you for working for what you want. You should be very proud of yourself. I'm pretty sure your mom is."

"So, you talked to my mom? For how long?"

"Oh, I don't know, half an hour or so."

"Oh my God, Jake, I just can't believe this. Look at you, you're a mess!"

"Well, thank you, you're not so bad yourself."

They both laughed.

"So, lunch?"

"I'd be delighted."

"Oh yeah, one more thing. I had told my office all about you and every year they give a deserving person who rises above all others a grant that pays for their tuition for four years of college to study journalism. And, depending on their grades when they graduate, they'll have an entry-level job for you at the paper. And this year, that person is you."

Jasmine stood in disbelief at what Jake had just told her. She quickly sat in the chair next to him and putting her hands over her face, cried as softly as she could not wanting to draw any attention from the people still in the room. Fortunately, one of the reporters had come out to take the calls for Jasmine – Jake had planned ahead and called to set this all up. Gently wrapping his arm around her, she turned to Jake and cried into his shoulder.

"I'm thinking you are happy about this?" He smiled as she looked into his deep blue smiling eyes. All she could do was nod.

"Great, now can we go have lunch, I'm starving!"

◄ 142 ►

Ten Storied Buildings
The Card Shop

Helen held the birthday card in her hand. She turned it over and there was the Hallmark stamp, signifying the best in greeting cards. She read the greeting inside, a generic greeting wishing the receiver a happy birthday and hoping that all their dreams come true. She loved the family ones because the greetings always spoke to the receiver as if they knew all about them and their special relationship to the sender. But Helen knew it wasn't true for everyone. She knew there were relatives that just did not get along, that were not 'the best and most generous brother' a person could have. She knew that a mother wasn't always 'the most loving and supportive mom in the world'. If she had had ambitions beyond owning a greeting card store for these forty-two years, she might have created her own line of greeting cards that told the truth about how self-centered, abusive, and just plain mean-spirited people can be. Sure, there are some perfect human beings out there, but there are also many who didn't quite match the words in all the beautiful cards that Helen sold in her shop. She would watch customers pick up one card, and then put it down and pick up another card, and after reading the greeting inside, maybe smiling – or, was it a smirk – they'd put the card back on the shelf and go onto the next one. Again and again, they just couldn't find the card with the right sentiment.

Helen would sometimes work her way toward a person, straightening out or adding new cards when a popular card was running low on the shelf. She would try to get a feel for whether or not they were the type of person who could use a little help or if they just wanted to keep reading the cards. She found that with the humorous cards, people just liked to read them. And more often than not, the humorous ones appealed to them and that was the one they settled on. Perhaps because the emotion was light and not something that pulled at a person's heart strings, causing them grief just reading the card and possibly remembering the pain the individual caused them.

Helen got into the greeting card business when she was just a teen, working at a Hallmark store. She was idealistic and loved the happy and loving sayings that appeared on the cards. They always made her smile and she imagined sending them to her loved ones or receiving them from people who loved her. She was living in her own fantasy world at the time, pretending that everything in her life was perfect and her family loved her, they just had a hard time showing it. Or they were having a bad day, or they were sad, or lonely, or confused about their lives and Helen just caused them more stress sometimes. She would try to stay out of her mom's way on those days and keep herself busy by helping around the house, making dinner, and cleaning up after, even though she had her own homework to do. It wasn't until years later that she found out, when her mom was finally diagnosed with bipolar disorder, that it wasn't Helen's fault at all. She hadn't been in the way or caused her mom to get upset or angry, and it wasn't her fault her mom had behaved as she did. But when you are burdened with these kinds of emotional responsibilities when you are a child, it is hard to shake them and they just cling to your heart far into your adult life, sometimes creating a crack that slowly widens over time, making it nearly impossible for any human to get close to you or for you to learn how to love, especially if you've never been taught how to love.

Most people just assume that you are taught about love by your parents. But what do you do if you didn't have loving parents? How do you learn? From a spouse? What if you meet and marry someone who isn't loving or, like you, didn't have loving parents either? Or is love just a part of us, in us, waiting to be released when we meet the right person? Or, if you meet a person who wasn't taught about love, can you both learn over time while getting to know each other about love and grow close and be happy together?

Helen wasn't sure about any of this because she'd never met someone she was willing to give her heart to for fear they would break it, or even worse, just not love her enough. Or not be able, or patient enough, to teach her about love. When she let her mind wander and imagine what it might have been like being in love, she was sometimes overwhelmed by sadness and would go to the section in the store where the humorous cards were. They were always there to snap her out of her downward spiraling moods. After reading just a few of them, she would begin to smile and sometimes even laugh out loud. If there was a customer browsing in her shop, she would sometimes even share the card with them. Several times they even liked the card so much they bought it. And this would always start a conversation with the person, sharing other funny cards that they had received and Helen showing them maybe another one or two that she knew always lifted her spirits.

For years this was how she kept her shop going. And it was successful. Particularly during the holiday seasons. But birthdays, weddings, and anniversaries brought many people to her shop throughout the year with her customers often commenting on how she had the very best selection. Sometimes they couldn't find a card for a niece or nephew but they found it at Helen's shop. It pleased her that she had so many satisfied customers. And regulars, too, that she came to know with some even becoming friends over the years.

Like Georgia, who she met the first day she opened her shop. A pretty woman, about her age when she'd opened, Georgia told her up front that she was a stay-at-home mom. But she was bored, looking for something to do with her time now that her kids were all in school, even though they were still young. "They don't need me so much now. I need a hobby. But I would really like a job. Just part time, you know, so I can be home when the kids get home from school." So, Helen hired her. They'd been together all of these years and had become the best of friends. Although Georgia was married when they'd first met, Helen wasn't sure how happy she was. Georgia had never talked much about her husband and Helen had wondered if he was just the one who paid the bills and not actually a partner in life. The care of the kids was mostly Georgia's responsibility. And then, about ten years ago, Georgia had come into work in tears. Although Helen had just opened the store for the day, she turned the sign to 'Closed' and walked with Georgia to the back room.

"What is it, what's wrong?" Helen suspected spousal physical abuse but Georgia had never come into work with bruises. She was almost positive there was some kind of verbal abuse, though.

"He's leaving me. Twenty-five years together and he's leaving me. For another woman. I gave him everything. Our two children, a beautiful home, the best home-cooked meals after teaching myself with cookbooks how to be a great cook. And love, whenever he needed it, I was there for him. I asked him what 'this woman' gave him that I didn't and he said, you know what he said, he said, 'she talks to me'. Like he thinks I don't want to talk. Sometimes I was so bored at night I almost called you up to ask, on those nights you were open a little later, if you wanted me to work. But he would just turn the TV on and read his paper and I got nothing from him. Nothing." Georgia let the tears out and Helen tried to console her as best she could.

"What am I going to do, Helen? What am I going to do?"

"Is he making you leave your home?"

"No, he said I can have the home. It is all paid for, I just have taxes, monthly utilities, upkeep, that kind of thing. He already cleaned out his drawers, his closet. He doesn't care about any of the material things. All the things that made up our lives."

"Well, they are just material things. Having each other is more important than any of that. And your children, of course." Helen knew she wasn't really helping. Since she never married, she just didn't know all the connections people made over the years that kept them together.

Georgia was quiet for a while then looked at Helen, tears dragging mascara down her cheeks.

"You never married. Did you not meet the right guy? We never talked much about that. I felt it was too personal and thought if you wanted to share, you would have. I think you were probably better off not giving your heart to someone. If you did, it might just have been broken by them. It was safer your way."

Helen thought about what Georgia was saying. And she was right, it was safer. But what was the payment for not having given her love and then be loved back? The risk was that the other person might not love her enough. That she already knew about herself. But maybe, just maybe, the reward would be to find someone to love her totally and completely, to share her life with them instead of the 'friends' she made working for forty-two years. And yes, besides Georgia, there were other couples Helen had become very close with and went to dinner with, always feeling like a third wheel.

There was one woman, Gloria, who thought Helen was gay while she thought she was just making another friend. Gloria visited the store about once a week and then she came several times a week and then almost daily. They talked and Helen really liked her. Gloria asked her to dinner and they had a fun time, laughing and sharing family stories. Gloria wasn't married either so Helen didn't have to hear stories about the kids and the grand kids which could sometimes go on for hours. Helen shared stories about her dogs and cat but it wasn't quite the same thing. Mostly the people just wanted to talk about their kids and Helen was a good listener. She did limit her time out with those people though. But Gloria had pets, no kids, no husband. Perfect. Until after the third time they went out to dinner and she invited Helen up to her apartment. They were enjoying an after-dinner cordial, relaxing on the couch, listening to some classical music, when Gloria made her move, causing Helen to throw her drink up in the air and jump up from the couch.

"What are you doing?" Helen started fanning herself, pacing while Gloria cleaned up the spilled drink.

"What does it look like I'm doing? I'm trying to seduce you, Helen."

"Seduce me? Why would you do that?"

"Because I really like you. And I thought you felt the same about me."

"I do really like you, Gloria. Just not sexually. I am heterosexual, not a lesbian."

"Then why did you go out with me, why so friendly? I kind of feel like you led me on, Helen."

"What to you is leading you on is just being a friend to me. I'm sorry we got our messages mixed up. And sorry if you feel I led you on. I was just looking for a friend, which I hope we can still be."

"Sure, of course we can." But after that night, Gloria stopped coming to the store. Helen did see her once around town with another woman. She hoped she had found what she was looking for.

Helen thought again about what Georgia had said when her husband had left her about making the safe choice. Reflecting back on that time caused Helen to reevaluate her whole life. Had she done the right thing? Was protecting her heart from feeling any pain, at the risk of maybe never feeling a love that could be great, worth it? How would she know, how could she know? Seeing her friend in pain after losing a husband that she'd had for twenty-five years, they must have had some good times over all those years. But from what Georgia had shared with her, she'd just married the wrong man. It didn't sound like they had much of a relationship, certainly not a close one. So, Georgia was just for sex and kids and taking care of the house. She had heard that before, how some men can't 'do' certain things with their wives because they are the mother of their children so they find a prostitute to have kinky sex with instead of trying different sex positions with their wives. That is a really messed up way of thinking, but it sounds like that might have been the case with Georgia's husband. Helen knew she'd never put up with that. Of course, she'd decided she didn't want kids and she'd met several men who, when they found out she wasn't interested in having a family, quickly dumped her. Apparently, they saw no future with her. Helen looked for that one guy who would love her for herself and not because he wanted her to have his babies. But she just never found him. And then she just stopped looking. Of course, now, whatever man she met would be older and have grown children. So, it wouldn't even be an issue. But it all took so much time, trying to find someone you are compatible with and who likes the same things you do and doesn't want to spend all of his time with his kids and grand kids, which wouldn't work for Helen either. No, she was better off on her own. She could meet and go out with a variety of female friends and even a couple of male friends that she'd met at the local Humane Society where she volunteered. One, she found out later, was married so she stopped going out with him. He'd said his wife was fine with it. It felt like cheating to Helen and she didn't want any part of it. The other man would talk mostly about himself and rarely asked Helen anything about herself. Maybe it was time to move to another state. Maybe start a new life. When she thought about Georgia and the question she'd asked about meeting the right guy, Helen would have a different answer today than the one she'd had ten years ago. Her answer today would be, no, she'd never met the right guy. She was almost positive that ten years ago she'd said she did but it just didn't work out. Helen would have been referring to one of the men who wanted children. She did think he was the right one. But when he contacted her nearly forty years later after finding a woman who wanted to bear his children and having three of them, he wanted to connect with Helen again. He was a cheater and Helen despised this kind of man. She knew he was a cheater even when she was with him that many years ago but didn't want to see it. And when he suggested they go away together now, with him still married to his wife, she told him he was a cheat and she wasn't interested in giving a cheat any of her time and to never call her again.

Georgia, of course, had found another man and was happy with this one. She shared her love life with Helen, even though Helen never asked. It seemed as if Georgia needed to confirm to herself that she'd been cheated out of the love and caring that she never got in her marriage. Helen was happy for her, although they did see each other less often than they used to. And, of course, Georgia had retired from working at Helen's store when she met her new man; he was financially set and Georgia was comfortable, too. They did a lot of traveling, something they were both interested in doing. They were thinking of moving to Norway but it wasn't definite. Georgia wasn't sure she wanted to move so far from the states.

"So, have a place in both countries." Helen figured she could see her friend at least half of the year.

"But that is so far away to have a second home."

"How would it be different from someone having a home in New Hampshire and a home in Florida."

"Because we could drive to Florida if we had to go there for an emergency."

"So, you fly to Norway if you had to for an emergency." Helen knew she was winning this one.

"But the cost is a little different."

"Oh, and you and Martin can't afford it?" Helen had her now, Georgia didn't have a good response and they both smiled and started to laugh.

"Who knows, since I'm retiring, too, maybe I'll move to Norway." Helen knew that was unlikely, but she really didn't have any plans now so anything was possible.

Georgia's eyes lit up but then she just shook her head when Helen started laughing.

"Well, anything is possible. I wouldn't rule it out."

Helen sold her store and made a fantastic retirement settlement for herself. The person who bought it reminded her of herself; a young woman who had worked at a Hallmark store and wanted her own store. Helen told her everything she could about the business, even staying a month until the new owner, Sandy, could handle everything herself. She even introduced her to many of the locals letting them know at the same time that she was retiring. The days went by quickly and soon the month was over and Helen gave Sandy her set of keys to the store and gave her a big hug, wishing her all the luck in the world. Sandy seemed unsure of the finality of the good-bye and looked for some reassurance from Helen that she would still be around.

"You will stop in to visit, won't you? Or buy a card or two, or a candle, a gift of some kind? But mostly for a visit?"

Helen wanted to reassure the young woman but knew she couldn't give her false hope and she certainly was not one to lie.

"I really don't know what I'm going to do, Sandy. I might be around next week, next month, even next year or until the day I die. I really do not have any plans. I've thought about it so many times but I cannot say for sure what I'll be doing. I've never had this luxury before so this is going to take more thinking than just the past few months that I've spent thinking about this decision.

But I can tell you this, for the time that I will still be around, I promise I will stop in when I can. Ok?"

That seemed to satisfy Sandy and she let out a big sigh and gave Helen a final parting hug.

For a couple of weeks, Helen got into the routine of going to the local bagel shop for a cup of English Breakfast tea with honey and cream and a lightly toasted plain bagel with vegetable cream cheese. She brought a book she was reading and thoroughly enjoyed the quiet of the shop and the smells of the coffees and breakfast sandwiches with fresh vegetables and eggs that were ordered each morning. From time to time, she would put her book down and observe the comings and goings of the morning rush. Several people, of course, would stop by to chat, some staying longer than Helen was comfortable with so she got into the habit of picking up her book after a while and hoped they would take the hint. Some did, others needed more of a hint and then Helen would pack up saying she had some errands to do and had to leave. But mostly, people respected her space and many would give her a wave, unless she called them over to chat.

There was one man, Helen had seen him when he came to her card store many times over the years. He was always so kind and gentle and seemed to want to talk to Helen more but they were often interrupted by other customers. She wasn't even sure if he was buying cards that he really needed or if he just wanted to buy something so he could talk to Helen. She didn't know if he was married so didn't engage in conversation beyond being polite and helpful. He always paid in cash so she hesitated to ask his name, just in case he was in a relationship. He did come by when she first announced in the local paper that she was retiring to wish her the best of luck in her travels, wherever they may take her. And now he started showing up in the bagel shop. When she first saw him, but he didn't see her, she didn't know what to do so she focused on her novel. He seemed to hesitate when he saw her, but then left the shop without speaking to her. She thought she was just being immature so decided if she saw him again, she would speak to him. If he was married, he'd always come to her store alone and now, again, she was seeing him alone at the bagel shop.

Several weeks went by and she actually looked, every day, for the good-looking man. And yes, he was good-looking. She thought he might be about her age, retired, also, since he came at different times in the morning. Helen was about to give up on seeing him again when one morning he walked in, carrying a book. He looked around the shop and when he spotted Helen, he gave her a nod and a smile. This time she gave him a smile back and waved him over. He held up a finger, indicating he would get his coffee and then head her way. Helen quickly checked her reflection in her mirror and deciding 'what you see is what you get', she put her mirror away. The man, taller than she remembered, pulled a chair out and sat in the seat closest to Helen.

"Good morning, Helen. How are you? It is nice to finally have a chance to talk to you. I can't tell you how long… anyway, I hope you are well." The man chattered on for a bit, obviously nervous, which Helen thought was very sweet. After a little small talk, Helen finally asked what she had been wondering for so long.

"In the many years that you came by in my store, you always paid for your purchases with cash so I was never able to find out your name. And I didn't want to ask and seem too forward if you were a married man. And I'm assuming, now, that you aren't married?"

The man shook his head. "I am not. And my name is Jacob, Jacob Durham." Jacob continued telling Helen his story and the hours passed. He didn't seem to be hesitant to share anything about his life with her. He made his money in the stock market and retired ten years ago. He has a house in town, one in North Carolina, and a cabin in Bar Harbor on the water.

"So, you were married?"

"Briefly, my wife had an incurable form of cancer. And this was many years ago, they have made so many advances over the years, who knows if they may have been able to save her if it happened now."

"But you never remarried?"

"Never found anyone I wanted to spend my life with. I dated, sure, but there was never that one. Well, there was one, but I just didn't know if she was interested in me. So, I never pursued it. You know the saying, it's better to remain silent and be thought a fool than to speak and remove all doubt. Or something like that. But I didn't know if she was married or had a man in her life, so I didn't pursue it. There was something about her, though, that I had never felt with anyone else. She always made me feel so comfortable to be around her. And she had the most amazing smile. And her hands were always so warm."

"Well, that is sad. You shouldn't let those opportunities pass you by. You just never know."

"Which is why I decided that I was going to take my chances and hope she was as interested in me as I am in her. Helen, would you go out to dinner with me?"

Ten Storied Buildings
The Office Building

An ambitious young man and willing to do whatever was
necessary to rise to the top in the corporate world, Dan found
himself working late into the night when all of the other employees
at J.P. Morgan had gone home. But Dan had read all the books
about getting to the top in whatever industry you chose and he
knew that working nine-to-five was never the way to make it. So, at
thirty-one, he knew he was on the right path and would continue
for as long as it took. As long as it didn't take ten more years. He
did have a timeline in mind; he was determined to be a millionaire
by the age of forty. He had nine more years and after working at
J.P. Morgan right out of college, after taking off a year to travel
around Europe learning French and Spanish along the way, he was
at the half-way mark. He was ready to take the next step forward.
The youngest to make account executive at twenty-six, he was
concerned that the company might be happy with him sitting
where he was for several more years. But he was getting antsy. He
needed to move up. He was ready to move into a vice president
position and didn't understand how he hadn't yet been given that
position. He was positive the company wouldn't be so careless to
not consider the best moves to make for the company. And if they
were looking out for the company, they would surely be
considering the next senior executive to promote to the status
position of VP. He had brought billions into the company already;
he knew his worth. He marked his calendar to talk to his boss

about his frustration and how they were disrupting his future, not in those words exactly but he would make his point clear.

Bank of America had contacted him several times and three years ago he even met with one of the senior principles at the Bank, who flew him down to Charlotte, and took him out to one of the finest restaurants in the city. Although it was a beautiful city, he knew he didn't want to leave New York, so after serious consideration, he declined their generous offer. His plan was to make it at J.P. Morgan. But there were times when he wondered if he'd made the right move, staying where he was.

Carrie loved her job. She loved working in the city of New York and loved the atmosphere of busy-ness that floated throughout the office. People were coming and going, papers being shuffled around, meetings held in various conference rooms around the company. Important people were escorted into these meetings, the secretaries brought urns of coffee and ordered full trays of varied breakfast and fresh-baked items. But New York had the best delis and bakeries in the world so finding premium food was never a problem. A local catering company was at their service whenever they needed them.

Carrie was one of the secretaries whose job was to set up meetings for the account executive she worked for. An older gentleman, George was the most considerate boss she could have imagined. He never let her carry anything that was the least bit heavy, ordering one of the interns to handle any lifting Carrie needed done. George often told her that she reminded him of his very busy daughter who had moved to France right after she received her undergraduate degree to attend the Paris College of Art. He obviously missed her tremendously and flew there with his wife as often as he could. He also had a son who hadn't found his way yet, having dropped out of college and now working at a bookstore last he heard. He didn't talk about him as much. But he wished the best for his son and hoped he found his passion before it was too late.

Because he was one of the senior account executives and was in high demand with their clients, George often had more work for Carrie than a lot of the other account executives. Except for Dan. Dan Bristol was always working, always there, the last to leave at night and first to arrive in the morning. Carrie couldn't imagine being his assistant. But she often found herself alone at night with Dan. She needed to prepare for the next day so sometimes stayed until the cleaning people showed up. She even started bringing a change of clothes if there was a particularly busy day on her calendar, knowing she wouldn't have time to get home, sleep, shower, and get back to work on time. George always left a stash of cash for her if she needed to take a taxi home, which he insisted. And of course, if she stayed, she could stash her clothes in his private bathroom and shower there before he arrived at work. He even let her sleep in his office. His only rule was that she had to be up and showered and out of his office by the time he arrived, usually around 7:30.

And then there was the big move coming up. Since a new building was under construction with completion due in a few short months, everyone was on edge as to what the new offices would look like. Prestige would come with what floor you were on. Since the building they were currently in was just a temporary location, few paid much attention to that. But the new high-rise offices would bring a whole new set of jealousy and envy. Carrie wasn't the least bit concerned about things like this and never participated in the gossip around the watercooler or in the ladies' room. She refused to spend her time with such pettiness. She only wanted to perform at her best and expected rewards for a job well-done. And George was the best boss at praising her work. She was a professional and always behaved that way. Shy and a bit withdrawn, she knew some of the other assistants gossiped about her, too, even though she never gave them any reason. She chose to rise above the small talk. She was also slim and attractive which gave the gossip group just one more thing to be jealous of. She also didn't join them when they went out drinking after work. A couple of them had asked her but when she kept refusing, they gave up. She usually preferred the company of a book to loud nightclubs with young executives hitting on her even though she wasn't interested in their advances. She was quite sure their only goal was to get her into bed. For one night. She knew a bar was not the place where she would find the love of her life.

No, she had other plans for finding 'the one'. Her soulmate. Her forever person. Her be all to end all, the father of her children, if that was what they decided, and someone to grow old with. She turned her attention to Dan's office. His head down as his fingers ran across the keyboard. Then pacing in his large office, speaking in Spanish or French to a client. He was in his element, where he was the most at ease, making deals. Carrie was sure what she felt was love, although she told herself it was admiration for such a strong, confident man. He was so self-assured and she was sure he never made any mistakes, which was how he had worked himself up to the top-producing senior executive in the office. She was positive he didn't even know she existed. Not in the same way she thought of Dan, anyway. She didn't know if he was married but she couldn't imagine a woman putting up with his hours at the office. Like herself, she doubted he had another life outside of work.

But then, at times like these when she was sitting, staring at Dan, watching his every move, imagining him as her lover, herself as his wife, watching him pace, he would turn and see her staring at him. Which would snap her out of her daydream and she would quickly return to her own computer and the work she was doing before she found herself distracted by Dan. Again.

No matter how hard Dan tried to leave the office at a reasonable time, and to him reasonable meant before 9pm, it rarely happened. He knew his long days into nights is what ended it with Daphne. The perfect complement to his Harvard degree, they had met at a sorority party. A Wellesley graduate, and part of the Alpha Kappa Alpha selective group of students, Daphne was brilliant and had political aspirations for herself. Finding the perfect man was part of her carefully designed life plan, too. And Dan had fit the bill. They were both addicted to work and success. Until Daphne wasn't any more. She had forgotten about the biological clock until it started going off in the middle of sex, in the middle of the night, in the middle of a meeting, always when she least expected it. And it was getting louder. And there seemed to be nothing she could do about it. Whenever she approached the subject of 'marriage and babies', and yes, they always went together, to Dan, he would change the subject and talk about a new client he was working with or the details of a meeting he'd had with his boss or one of the other senior executives. He just was not interested and wondered why she had to bring this up when everything between them was going so smoothly and, in his mind, they were right on track.

And so, it ended. Dan was upset at first; they had been together for seven years, but he also understood what Daphne wanted and knew he couldn't give her that. He wasn't even sure he wanted children, knowing his wife and the kids would suffer. Sure, he could give them every material thing they could ever dream of, but he knew that kids needed their dad's attention and time. He just didn't know if he could give a child, even one child, any of that.

So, after their breakup, he dove deeper into his work. Now there was nothing holding him back from advancing from the top senior executive to become the next in line for a vice-presidency in the company.

What did he miss from his relationship with Daphne? If he was honest with himself, he missed the sex, which was great. When he could focus on it. He was often distracted; they would sometimes both share work situations and more recently with Daphne it was all about marriage and babies. But the sex worked, mostly. Sometimes when he was in the office late, he would catch the assistant who worked for George, Dan's personal hero, looking at him like she was in a daydream. He tried smiling but when she saw him looking back at her she would quickly turn away and return to her computer. He decided to find out what she was all about. She certainly was attractive and had an awesome body. Maybe they could go out. They were both often working late at the office so maybe a dinner out would be nice for a change. Definitely, dinner and dessert was exactly what he needed.

Dan had a plan. He knew sometimes Carrie delivered reports from George to the other Senior Executives. He would put the ball in her court. He had the opportunity the very next day when Carrie brought in the previous day's reports. Dan was busy working on a schedule and looked up when Carrie walked in. He had never noticed before but he was positive she always blushed when he looked up. He looked at her and said thank you when she put the report on his desk. She smiled, and turned to walk through his seating area to the door. Although the office was all glass, he had the option of closing blinds if he wanted privacy. His office was one of the larger ones and he preferred his desk all the way down at one end so when someone entered, they had a long walk to his desk. With floor to ceiling windows, his office had an expansive view of the city. It was gorgeous, particularly at night.

"I need you." Barely a whisper.

Carrie hesitated but didn't turn and continued walking out of his office.

When she got back to her desk she waited a few minutes and then turned towards Dan's office. He was deep in concentration and then, right when she was looking at him, he looked at her. And he smiled. She quickly looked away and busied herself at her desk.

Had she imagined that he said, 'I need you'? She couldn't concentrate. All she could think about was what she was positive Dan had just said to her. Or did he? Did she hear what she thought she heard? He couldn't have said that. She's thinking crazy thoughts now, why would he say that to her. He'd never given her any indication that he had any feelings for her. Why now? Didn't he have a girlfriend? She recalled having heard some gossip when she was in the ladies' room about him breaking up with her. Her name was, a 'D' name, Doreen, something exotic, Delilah, Daphne… Daphne, that was it. That sounded right. An ivy-league uppity name. She was sure that's the kind of woman Dan would be with, would marry and have kids with, someone to elevate his social position, from a wealthy family no doubt. Would he ever be interested in someone who came from modest wealth, like Carrie? She had a mom who worked at a ladies' clothing store and a dad who was a high school teacher. Nothing fancy. Would he, could he, be interested in her? She shook these thoughts out of her head and got back to work.

The next day and the day after, Carrie distributed the reports from her boss George as usual. George was old school and believed in the printed daily report. It was a mere five pages, but he required all the senior executives to physically sign off on them so none of them could claim they'd never received it, which sometimes happened with reports sent electronically. Again, as Carrie was leaving Dan's office, she heard him say:

"I need you."

On the fourth day, she was done with this and when she heard those words, "I need you", she turned and walked back towards Dan's desk.

"What did you say?"

Dan, surprised that she'd gone several days without saying a word, was caught off-guard and tried to pretend he hadn't said anything, shaking his head as she walked towards him.

"I, um, I didn't…"

"Let me refresh your memory. You said, 'I need you'." Where this courage was coming from surprised Carrie as much as it seemed to surprise Dan. But Dan, smooth guy that he was, quickly found his composure and, with a sly smile, nodded at Carrie, leaned back in his chair, while Carrie stood directly in front of his desk, and waited. He could see she was starting to lose her confidence, watching her face turn a light shade of pink. He was enjoying her being uncomfortable for just a minute and when she started to turn to leave, he stood up.

"I'm sorry."

"Wait. You're right. I did say that. I wondered how long it was going to take you to respond to me. Or if you ever would. But I'm glad you finally did."

Carrie faced him now and, although her cheeks were a brighter shade of pink, she managed to also smile at Dan.

"So, now that we are officially speaking to each other, would you like to go to dinner with me?"

"Yes, I'd like that."

"I could take a break for an hour or so, how about around seven?"

"That sounds great. I'll see you then."

At 6:45, Carrie was so excited she could barely touch up her makeup without smearing it a little. In ten minutes, she felt refreshed and ready for her dinner date. She walked over to Dan's office and was surprised to see him on the phone, looking out his windows at the city lights, relaxed in his chair as if he was settling in for a long conversation. Carrie lightly knocked on the door and walked inside. He didn't turn to her. He didn't even seem to notice that she'd come into his office. She sat in one of his chairs in the seating area in the middle of his office. She waited about fifteen minutes and then he turned and saw her sitting there. He put his hand over the phone and after catching his breath from laughing with whoever was on the other end of the phone, he motioned for her to sit out at her desk.

"I'll just be five more minutes. It's an old friend, we're catching up. Five minutes."

Sitting at her desk Carrie thought about putting her computer back on but Dan did say five minutes. Five minutes. And now she had waited nearly twenty-five minutes and he wasn't making any effort to get off the phone. He never even looked her way. Finally, after nearly an hour, he did turn in his chair and caught sight of her, looking surprised to see her sitting there and then as if remembering about their dinner date, stood up and said his good-byes to his 'old friend'. He grabbed his jacket, excused himself to use the men's room and came back in five minutes.

"Ok, ready?"

"Yes, I am."

They got in the elevator going down to the garage. She followed him to his car, a Porsche, of course. This wasn't starting off quite the way Carrie imagined. She was hoping it would get better from here.

He made only small talk on the drive to the restaurant, asking her if she liked her job, how long she'd worked there now, had she gone to college and what was her major. It was feeling more like a job interview than finding out if you liked someone or had anything in common with them. He did ask if she had a boyfriend and seem relieved when she said 'no'. Like him, she joked, she spent the better part of her life working. She did enjoy reading. She thought that might engage him in a conversation, but he didn't even ask what she liked to read. She was having serious doubts about their future together.

At the restaurant she'd barely read the menu and he was ordering for both of them.

"But you don't know what I like. How can you order for me?"

"It's Filet Mignon. Of course you'll like it. Who doesn't?"

"I might be a vegetarian."

He laughed.

The champagne, that he also ordered without consulting with her, arrived and after the waiter poured them each a flute, Dan raised his glass. Carrie wondered what on earth they would be toasting. She was hoping to a better evening. She decided to humor him and clinked his glass.

"To a beautiful night." Carrie started to drink but he wasn't finished. He held his glass up waiting for her to put hers back up to his so he could continue.

"And a rewarding one." And he winked, smiling from ear to ear. Carrie naively wondered what he meant but she didn't bother to ask. She was sure this would be their one and only date. Whether or not it was 'rewarding' he certainly would never find out since after dinner she was going to ask him to take her back to her apartment. He would undoubtedly be going back to work. The reward for him was going to be having an hour or so of her company. She had already decided she didn't even want to give him a kiss good-night.

The meal was delicious and after the bubbly worked its magic, she was feeling a little giggly. She tried asking him about his life but he wasn't interested in sharing.

"Weren't you engaged for a while?"

"Engaged? No, not even close." He watched her eat and seemed to be hurrying her along. She even caught him checking his watch.

After the champagne was gone, he never asked if she wanted dessert but called for the check. No dessert, no coffee or tea, just the check.

"Are you in a hurry to go someplace?" The champagne gave her the courage to ask whatever came into her mind.

He laughed.

"You might say that." He swallowed the rest of his champagne.

He paid the check and then stood up to leave. She followed behind to the elevators.

In the garage, he hopped in his car and off they went.

"Wait, I have to tell you where I live."

"Yes, yes, that's better. What is the address? Wait, do you have a roommate?"

"No. Why? What difference would that make."

"Just asking." He put the address in his GPS and off they went. It was after 10pm so the traffic was minimal and they got there in less than twenty minutes. Carrie jumped out of his car and was thanking him for the meal when he also got out of the car. So, what, now he's going to be gallant and walk her to her door?

"So, thank you for a delicious dinner, Dan. And I'll see you at work." And Carrie started to turn to her building when Dan grabbed her and kissed her hard on the lips. She quickly pulled away.

"What are you doing? Did it sound like I wanted a kiss from you?"

"What are you doing? Do you think I just spend two-hundred and fifty dollars and not even get a kiss? Which comes nowhere near what I was expecting. Even a blow job is the least I should get for tonight."

Carrie stood with her mouth open, eyes wide, appalled at the words coming out of Dan's mouth. Never did she expect this kind of behavior from the work obsessed man she'd pined over for the past several months.

"But, you need me. You said it several times. You need me."

"Yes, I need you. What do you think that meant? I'll tell you what it meant. It meant what I was expecting to get tonight, sex, in several positions, many orgasms for me, for several hours. Yes, I need you to have sex with me."

Again, Carrie stood staring at this man like she was seeing him for the first time, and not for all the months when they both worked in the same office, staying late when so many others had left hours ago, and it was just the two of them. How many times did he say 'I need you'? How could she be so wrong about his intentions?

"Oh no, no, no. What did you think I meant? Like you are my soulmate and we would start this wonderful romance and maybe get married and have three or four kids and have a gorgeous home in the burbs? Is that what you thought? Oh my God, that's what you thought." Again, he laughed. He shook his head, leaned against his car, laughing. Carrie wanted to slap his laughing face so hard. She was about to raise her hand when he grabbed it and placed it on his crotch.

"Ok, tell you what, how about a blow job. And we'll call it even."

She pulled her hand away.

"You disgust me. Get away from me or I'll scream."

Dan looked up and down the street and saw a couple walking towards them.

"You're a dick-tease, that's what you are." Dan opened his car door to get in.

"And you are a sad, pathetic man."

Carrie turned and walked towards her apartment building. As she went up in the elevator to her floor, she knew she would have to look for another job.

Acknowledgements

As always, I must thank first and foremost my amazing husband, Jim, for all the knowledge he has accumulated over the years both in the tech world and in the publishing business. If it wasn't for his expertise, I can't even imagine what my many books would look like. And, most likely, many would not even make it to the finished book stage.

Thank you to my friends, many who are also readers, for their continued support of my work. I appreciate it more than you will ever know.

About the Author

DJ Geribo, author and fine artist, lives in rural New Hampshire near Lake Winnipesaukee. After pursuing fine art for many years, she decided to focus on her writing and has published works across multiple genres.

Besides writing, which keeps DJ very busy, she also enjoys reading, of course, painting, exercise in many forms from lifting weights, e-bike riding, golfing in the summer with her husband, snowshoeing in the winter months, and walking any time of year. And she loves just hanging out with her Pomeranian and her Cockatoo.

DJ's books can be purchased directly from her website at www.DJGeribo.com as well as her Publisher's website at www.BBDPublishing.com. You can also ask for her titles at your favorite bookseller.

To learn about DJ's latest and forthcoming books, visit her website and join her e-mail list or visit BBD Publishing's website.

Other Books by DJ Geribo

Useful Pieces: Sean and Jill are just beginning to see their hopes and dreams fulfilled, having recently moved into a charming cottage that seems too good to be true. Looming above their new home is the grand mansion owned by the Charmeins, an aging couple who appear to know everything about them. Sean and Jill begin to suspect the Charmeins are behind the unsettling events that are steadily upending their lives, all to serve some hidden agenda. How two reclusive elderly people could orchestrate such chaos remains a disturbing mystery. The reason why soon becomes terrifyingly clear, driving Sean and Jill to plot a desperate revenge - one that ends with consequences neither of them could ever have imagined. Softcover - $17.95

Deep Lake House: A collection of stories based on the people who've visited Deep Lake House over the span of a century. All of their stories have made a lasting impression on the House, the main character and narrator. Some sad, some uplifting and joyful, all likely to make an impression on the reader, too. Softcover - $15.95

The Mart: A novel and collection of stories where the characters appear in both. Two main characters dominate the novel, while others have their starring roles in the individual stories. Together they complement each other in a world that can both break your heart and lift your spirits. Softcover - $17.95

Me & Them: A memoir like none you've ever read before. If you grew up during the nineteen-fifties and sixties you'll feel right at home in this collection of vignettes on daily life. Some will make you laugh while others may make you cry. But you won't read this collection without reminiscing about your own childhood. Softcover - $15.95

Seven Storied Houses: A house's facade isn't always a good indication of the kind of lives experienced by its occupants. A mansion doesn't mean a happy family any more than a much-in-need-of-repair home points to a life of misery. Both can be full of memories and only the occupants decide if they will be good or bad. Softcover - $15.95

Mouse Bound: A story that came about after a mouse set up residence in the author's studio. After live-catching and driving the mouse to another location, she imagined the adventures he'd have experienced in returning to the best and only home he'd ever known, back in her studio. Softcover - $10.95

The Miracle Dog: When the author's dog, Kameko, collapsed into her arms one summer morning, DJ knew something was very wrong. A trip to the vet confirmed a life-threatening diagnosis with DJ's precious Pomeranian spending nearly a week in an ICU at an emergency vet hospital that included four blood transfusions. After many daily trips back to the hospital, finally a combination of medicines saw DJ's beloved Pom back on the road to recovery. Softcover - $16.95

Eddie Easel and the Case of the Missing Green: A creative children's story that teaches a child the basics of art and painting all through an engaging mystery. A story any child will love and one that may even start your child on an artistic career path.
Hardcover - $17.95 – Exclusively through BBD Publishing

The House at the Top of the Trees: While riding their bikes, Nat and Devon spot a house that appears to be sitting at the top of a tree. Curiously, they find a way to get there and discover a world unlike anything they've ever known before, a place where all of their dreams come true. Is it safe to stay or should they return home to their hard-working single mom who does her best to support her children who mean the world to her? Softcover – $16.95

Coming Soon

The Castle at the Bottom of the Sea – The second middle grade adventure book featuring Nat and Devon (from The House at the Top of the Trees) that takes them to the shore and another exciting and surreal adventure.

My Neighbor, the Alien – Jeff and his best friend Wilt are sure Jeff's neighbor is an alien. But what is he doing in their neighborhood? And how does he know their teacher from school? It seems the real learning has just begun for the two curious boys.

All of DJ's book can be purchased directly from her Publisher at www.BBDPublishing.com

You may also ask for her titles from your favorite bookseller.

Select titles can be purchased on Amazon in paperback and Kindle editions.

Leave Us a Review

Did you like *Ten Storied Buildings*? BBD Publishing would love to hear your thoughts on this and any of the other books by author DJ Geribo that you've read.

Visit www.BBDPublishing.com and on the home page, click on the 'Submit A Comment' button in the right-hand column under the Readers' Comments. This will take you to the 'Submit Your Reader's Comments' form where you can share your comments about this or other books by DJ Geribo.

If you purchased this book on Amazon, please leave an Amazon Review to help other readers find and enjoy DJ's books.

Thank you for your interest in DJ Geribo's books.